D1535529

THE STORY OF ROLF
AND THE VIKING BOW

The Story of Rolf
And the Viking Bow

by Allen French

BETHLEHEM BOOKS · IGNATIUS PRESS
BATHGATE, N.D.   SAN FRANCISCO

Also by Allen French

FICTION

The Red Keep

The Lost Baron

Heroes of Iceland

The Story of Grettir the Strong

NON-FICTION

The Siege of Boston

First Year of the American Revolution

General Gage's Informers

Historic Concord and the Lexington Fight

To my brother,
Hollis French

ISBN 978-1-883937-01-0
Library of Congress Catalog Number: 93-72606

Bethlehem Books • Ignatius Press
10194 Garfield Street South
Bathgate, ND 58216
www.bethlehembooks.com

Printed in the United States on acid free paper

Manufactured by Thomson-Shore, Dexter, MI (USA); RMA583LS664, August 2012

Table Of Contents

THE STORY OF ROLF
AND THE VIKING BOW

Introduction

ALLEN FRENCH wrote this tale of Iceland—*The Story of Rolf and the Viking Bow*—in the early 1900's; Bethlehem Books is republishing it now because we think it deserves to be discovered by a new audience of readers. I was introduced to it myself when, one day, a young friend left his library copy around. I picked it up and couldn't put it down. Reading *Rolf* was somewhat like taking a drink of water straight from the glacier's source.

The novel is set around 1010 A.D., a generation or so after Christianity was introduced to the island—the same era as that in which Iceland's sagas take place. The sagas themselves were committed to writing at a later period, in the 12th and 13th centuries. They related the deeds of heroic figures from this early time, not a terribly distant past for the saga writers; a sharp sense of historical connection is evident in the many references to local places, family names, and to the institution of customs. How historical the heroes themselves are—Njal, Gisli, Grettir, and many others—is debated. Their greatness in literary terms, however, has many champions. There is no doubt of their place in heroic literature.

Allen French, like J.R.R.Tolkien, immersed his imagination in this ancient lore. Not all of us have the preparation or hardihood to do likewise. The terse, condensed narrative of the originals, with its unfamiliar worlds of reference, can make hard going for an ordinary modern reader. What we so appreciate about Mr. French's achievement is that he emerged from that world and gave us this exceptional and readable tale: *The Story of Rolf.*

A glance at the book's opening sentence tells much:

> In the time after Iceland had become Christian, and after the burning of Njal, but before the deaths of Snorri the Priest and Grettir the Outlaw, there lived at Cragness above Broadfirth a man named Hiarandi, called the Unlucky.

Here we have the flavor of authentic saga: direct, brief, exact, and concerned to establish a historical context. The character of Rolf (son of Hiarandi) is the author's own invention. But Rolf's destiny is woven into the broad pattern of history passed down to us in Iceland's sagas.

The novel draws us into those events beginning with the fateful act of Hiarandi's lighting a fire-beacon on his coastland cliff.

In this initiative Rolf's father challenges the status quo and—to save lives—risks his own and his neighbor's prosperity.

The Story of Rolf traces the costly consequences of his act of generosity. The conflict in this tale must be worked out not simply between opposing individuals, but between families. The Soursops, Rolf's family, and the family of Einar are at odds; the key to resolving the feud has a legal side to it, around which all the adventures play. But the personal side, as we proceed, grows more and more important. How will Rolf and Einar's son Grani come to terms?

Great development is given to the related themes of forgiveness and growth in character. In this respect the tale is true to the novels of our age, which focus on the inner life of the person. The final chapters of Rolf bring this focus to a climax. We ponder the wrong that must be righted, not by force nor shrewdness alone, but by longsuffering, patience, and meekness. French tells us in the preface to the original edition that for the closing incidents of his story, he drew upon a piece of writing from the early literature, "that wonderful fragment of Thorstein Staffsmitten," where "the spirit of those days is particularly well given." His manner of working with this fragment combines, to powerful advantage, the dramatic brevity of Icelandic speech and action with our latter-day sensitivity to moral development.

It's not just what is told, but how it's told that makes Rolf's story noteworthy. The texture of the writing embodies the time and place and people. It is characterized by uncluttered narration, curt dialogue full of compressed feeling, verbs shifting at times to the present tense to suggest heightened action, "skaldic" verse. The presence of these verse kernels is typical of the ancient sagas, which were written in prose, but contained short sections of stylized poetry. That poetry marked the heightened import of certain moments. They were reminders of the days when verse was recited orally by skalds (poets) and even extemporaneously by heroes. Thus, the verse marks dramatic moments in the dialogue: the characters turn to lines of deep-felt import in a style true to the Icelandic temper.

The author found personal interest in the Norsemen (the Icelander being one branch) who "represents, with slight differences, all the old nations of Teutonic stock," and whose customs, languages, and blood-lines have contributed so much to our modern English-speaking world. In these saga heroes French singled out the quality of courage "not the courage of the Greek [hero], to whom tears and flight are no disgrace, but the steadfastness in every stress of men dependent on themselves." *

Such is Rolf's steadfastness. It feeds a hunger in us. It quenches a thirst. Drink, then, fellow reader, from this Icelandic stream.

Lydia Reynolds
Bethlehem Books
Summer 1993

---

* Preface to his adaptation of *The Story of Burnt Njal* (Dasent's translation), published in 1926 as *Heroes of Iceland*.

Pronunciation Guide

(Adapted from French's *Heroes of Iceland*)

The simplest rule for a uniform pronunciation of Icelandic names is to treat all vowel and consonant sounds as if they were German. Thus, on the stressed syllable:

a has the sound of **a** in *far,* as in Kiartin
(pronounce "Kyartan")

e   "   **e** in *fed,* as in Grettir

ei   "   **i** in *pine,* as in Einar

i   "   **e** in *meet,* as in Gisli

o   "   **o** in *note,* as in Frodi

u   "   **u** in *pull,* as in Hrut

g   "   **g** in *get,* as in Gisli
(pronounce with hard **g**)

th   "   **t** in *tot,* as in Thord of
Laxriver; Althing

i, when it comes right after a consonant, is pronounced like "**y**" as in Kiartan (Kyartan)

I

Of the Lighting of the Beacon

IN THE TIME after Iceland had become Christian, and after the burning of Njal, but before the deaths of Snorri the Priest and Grettir the Outlaw, there lived at Cragness above Broadfirth a man named Hiarandi, called the Unlucky. And well was he so named, for he got a poor inheritance from his father, but he left a poorer to his son.

Now the farm of Cragness was a fertile fell, standing above the land round about, and girt with crags. Below lay Broadfirth, great and wide, and Cragness jutted out into it, a danger to ships. It had no harbor, but a little cove among the rocks, where Hiarandi kept his boat; and many ships were wrecked on the headland, bringing fortune to the owners of Cragness, both in goods and firewood. And all the land about once belonged to the farm. Rich, therefore, would have been the dwellers at Cragness, but for the doings of Hiarandi's father.

He would always be striving at the law, and he

was of ill judgment or ill luck, for what he gained at the farm he always lost. The older he grew, the more quarrelsome he became; and judgments heaped heavy on him, until at last he was so hard put that he must sell all his outlying lands. So the farm, from a wide estate, became only the land of Cragness itself, and another holding of a few acres, lying inland on the uplands, within sight of Cragness and the sea.

In the time when Hiarandi was young, Iceland was still heathen. He sought his fortune in a trading voyage, and sailed West-over-the-Sea, trading in the South Isles as a chapman, trafficking in goods of all kinds. And he made money there, so that at last when he sailed again for home he counted on a fair future. But the ship was wrecked in a storm, and few of the men came ashore; and Hiarandi himself was saved by means of a maid who dwelt at the place, who dragged him from the surf. So Hiarandi came home on foot, his clothes in tatters, having lost money rather than gained it. Then his father, whose losses pressed heavy on him, struggled no more with the world, but went to his bed and died. And in that summer when all Iceland took to the new faith, Hiarandi became master at Cragness.

Hiarandi was a silent man, not neighborly, but hard-working. An unworldly choice he made of a wife, for he took that woman who had saved him from the waves; she was the daughter of a small farmer and brought neither dowry nor kinship of any power. So men said that Hiarandi had no wish to rise in the world. He lived upon his farm, with two thralls and a bondservant; and husbanding his goods well, by little and little he made money which he put out at call, and so bade fair to do better than his father, for all his poor start in life. And a loving spouse he had in Asdis, his wife, who one day bore him a son.

They named the lad Rolf, and he grew to be well knit; he was not powerful, but straight and supple, and of great craft in his hands. And from delight in the boy Hiarandi changed his ways, and became more cheerful, going to fairs and meetings for the sake of Rolf. And Hiarandi taught the lad all he knew of weapon-craft, which was not a little. The lad was swift of foot; he was skilled in the use of the sword and javelin, but most he delighted in the use of the bow.

And that was natural, for upon the cliffs seabirds lived in thousands, hard to catch. The boy went down to their nests with ropes, and took eggs in their season, or the young before they could fly, and both for food. So skilled was he in this that he was called Craggeir, the Cragsman; and no man could surpass him, whether in daring or skill. But there were times when there were no eggs nor fledglings, and from his earliest boyhood Rolf practised in shooting with his bow at the birds, and he kept the larder ever full.

Happy was Hiarandi watching his son, and his pride in him was great. As the lad grew stronger, the father made for him stronger bows and heavier arrows, until at the age of fourteen Rolf used the bow of a man. Then one winter they went down together into the valley, father and son, and watched the sports and games on the frozen mere.

There the men of the place played at ball, and great was the laughter or deep was the feeling. Now Hiarandi would not let Rolf play, for often matters came to blows, and he would not have his son maimed. But when it came to shooting with the bow, Hiarandi put Rolf forward, and it was seen who was the best at that play. For though the men shot, Rolf surpassed them all, not in distance but in skill. He hit the smallest mark at the greatest distance; and when Hiarandi brought a pigeon and freed it, then Rolf brought it down. No one there had seen such shooting. Then those who were not envious named the lad Rolf the Bowman.

But a man named Einar stood by, and he lived on the land which Hiarandi's father had sold. He was rich but covetous, and fond of show, and fond of praise. There lived with him one named Ondott, an Eastfirther who had left his district and come west, a man without property. He stood with Einar and watched the games.

"See," said Einar, "how proud is Hiarandi of his son!"

"Thou hast a son as well," said Ondott. "How he

will shine among these churls when he returns from his fostering in the South Isles!"

"Aye," answered Einar. "Like an Earl will he be, and no farmer of these parts will compare with him."

"And as for the shooting of this lad," remarked Ondott, "it is not so fine after all."

"In the Orkneys," said Einar aloud, so that others should hear him, "they are better bowmen than here, and the Earl will have my son taught everything."

Now some who stood by brought Hiarandi this tale. "Have a care," said they. "Thy neighbor Einar sets himself above thee."

"Then he must set himself high," answered Hiarandi with a laugh, "for his land lies far lower than mine."

Then others carried that tale to Einar, and he laid it up in his mind; but Hiarandi forgot all that had been said, nor did he remember to tell of it to Asdis when they had returned from the games.

Then the winter passed on with severe storms, and ships were wrecked on Cragness rocks, but no men reached shore. And Einar envied the more the riches that came to Hiarandi from the wrecks, in firewood, timber, and merchandise. And once a whale came ashore, and that was great fortune. But one evening, as those at Cragness sat within the hall, Asdis came and stood beside her husband, and said, "Listen to the wind."

"There is no need to listen," said Hiarandi. "The wind howls for a storm, and this night will be bad."

Then Thurid the bondservant, who sat by the fire, looked up and said, "Ships are off the land."

"Hearest thou that?" asked Asdis in a low voice. "The woman is strange, but she forecasts well."

"Aye," answered Hiarandi, "it is likely that ships will be on the rocks by morning."

"Now," asked Asdis, "dost thou remember the time thou camest ashore, these many years ago?"

"How should I forget it?" responded Hiarandi.

"But no one can rush into the water here," said Asdis, "to save those who are wrecked."

"That is true," quoth Hiarandi. "I am sorry for the mariners, yet how is one to help?"

Then the bondservant raised her head and sang this song:

"The sea brings money;
Money is bonny.
Bless then the sea
Which brings good to thee."

After that she sat silent and sunken as before.

"Hear the hag," said Asdis, shuddering. "But we prosper through the misfortunes of others."

"What is to be done?" asked Hiarandi.

"It is in my mind," said Asdis, "that if we made a fire-beacon, people could steer from shore and so into safe harbor farther up the firth."

"Now," quoth Hiarandi, "that might be done."

"Wilt thou do it?" asked Asdis.

Then the woman raised her head and sang again:

"He is a fool
Who leaves old rule.
Set heart 'gainst head,
How then butter thy bread?"

Then Hiarandi said to Asdis: "No man has ever yet set beacons against shipwreck. All men agree to take the fortune of the sea; and what is cast on a man's beaches, that is his by old custom."

"Thinkest thou that is right?" asked Asdis.

"Moreover," went on Hiarandi, "the sea is but giving me again what it took away."

"Never can the sea," answered Asdis, "give thee true happiness through other men's misfortunes."

"Remember the boy," said Hiarandi. "Shall I leave him with nothing to begin the world with? For my own earnings bring me at most a mark of silver in the year."

"For all that," replied Asdis, "it is in my mind that to do otherwise were to do better. How canst thou have the heart that men should die longer on our rocks, and we not do our best to save them?"

Then Hiarandi, answering nothing, rose and paced up and down before the fire. And the carline sang once more:

"Take what is given.
No man is wise
Who asketh twice
If earth or heaven
Sends him his prize."

But Asdis stood upright, and she sang:

"Suffer not wrong
To happen long,
Lest punishment
From heaven be sent."

Now in Iceland all men loved the singing of skalds; but though Hiarandi had heard the carline sing many times before, never had he heard rhymes from his wife. So he stood astonished.

Then the bondservant sang again:

"Ill will attend
The beacon's lighting.
Bad spirit's guiding
Will bring false friend."

But Asdis sang with great vehemence:

"Let God decide
What fate shall ride
Upon the wind.
Be thou not blind
To duty's hest.
My rede is best.
List to the storm!
Go! Save from harm
The mariner
Whose fate is near.
To others do
As I did once to you."

And it seemed to Hiarandi as if she commanded him. Moreover, as he listened, the storm roared louder. Then he seized his cloak, and cried to his thralls, "Up, and out with me to make a beacon!"

Though they dared not disobey, they grumbled,

and they got their cloaks slowly. For they saw slipping away from them the fine pickings from the wreck, which brought them warm clothes and handsome. Out they went with Hiarandi into the storm, and kindled a great fire at the edge of the cliff. And Rolf toiled too; but Asdis did best of all, for she brought out in a kettle great strips of whale's blubber, and flung them on the fire. Then the flames flared high and wide, as bright as day. And Rolf sprang to the edge of the cliffs and gazed upon the water. Then, pointing, he cried, "Look!"

Down below was a ship; its sail flapped in rags, and the crew were laboring mightily at the oars to save themselves, looking with dread at the white breakers and the looming rocks. Now in the strength of their fear they held the vessel where she was; and by the broad light of the fire every man of them was visible to the Cragness-dwellers. To Rolf that was a dreadful sight. But the bit of a sail was set, and men ran to the steering-oar to hold the vessel stiff; and behold, she moved forward, staggered past the rocks, made clearer water, and wore slowly out into the firth. Even the thralls shouted at the sight.

Then Hiarandi left one of the thralls to keep the fire, and went back to the hall with those others. There the carline still sat.

"So he is safe past the rocks?" she asked, yet speaking as if she knew.

"Aye, safe," answered Hiarandi.

"Now," said she, "thou hast brought thy evil fortune

on thyself, and it will be hard to avoid the extreme of it."

"I care not," answered Hiarandi, "even though I suffer for a good deed."

"Nevertheless," said the carline, "the future may be safe, though without riches, if thou wilt be guided by me. Wilt thou follow my redes?"

"No advices of thine do I follow," replied Hiarandi. "For methinks thou still servest the old gods, and canst work witchcraft. Speak no more of this matter in my house; and practise not thy sorcery before my eyes, for the law gives death as punishment."

"Now," answered the woman, "like a foolish man, thou rushest on thy fate. And I see clearly that thou art not he who was spoken of in the prophecy. Not a fortunate Soursop art thou."

"Since the slaying of Kol, who put the curse on all our stock," answered Hiarandi, "has but one of the Soursops prospered. How then should I be fortunate?"

"Two were to prosper," the woman replied. "And each was to put an end to the curse in his branch of thy race. Snorri the Priest is one of those two, as all men know. But thou art not the other; and I believe that thou art doomed to fail, even as thy father was."

"So I have long believed," said Hiarandi calmly.

Then the carline rose, and her eyes were strange, as if they saw beyond that upon which she looked. "More misfortune is coming than thou deemest," she said. "Outlawry. Mayhap even death. Be warned!"

"Thou art a heathen and a witch," said her master. "Be still!"

But she said: "I will not abide the curse. Hiarandi, I have worked long in thy house. Give me now my freedom and let me go."

"Thou hast long been free to go," he replied. "Take thy croaking to another man's board! But this little prophecy I give to thee, that no man will believe thine ill-speaking."

"No great foresight hast thou in that," she answered. "Never have I been believed." Then she drew on her cloak and hooded her face.

"Thou will not go in the storm?" asked Asdis.

"All times are alike," the woman said. "Heed thou this, Hiarandi. Beware the man who came in the ship thou didst save!"

"He is one," answered Hiarandi, "whom I fear not at all."

"Beware suits at law," said the carline again, and she turned to go.

"It needs no great wisdom to say that," retorted Hiarandi upon her. "But stay! I send not people from my door penniless. Nothing is owing from me to thee, yet I will give a piece of money."

"Soon," answered Thurid, "thou wilt need all thou hast." And she went out into the night.

II

Of the Soursops, and the Curse which Hung on Them

OF THOSE THINGS which had been said, Rolf heard all, yet he had not spoken. Now he drew near to his father, and said to him: "Explain to me, father, the things of which the woman spoke. What is the curse upon us, and can such a thing be true?"

Then Hiarandi answered: "Thou knowest we are of the Soursops, who got their name when they sopped with sour whey the fire which was kindled to burn them in their house. Now Gisli, the first of us, slew Kol, his wife's foster-father, for the sake of his sword Graysteel, and Kol laid the curse of misfortune on us. Slayings arose by means of that sword; there came the outlawing of Gisli, the grandson of the first Gisli, and death fell in most branches of the house. Fourteen years Gisli was outlaw, even as has been, to this year, Grettir the Strong, who is the great outlaw of our day. But Gisli was slain, and his brother, while his sister died. Son of that sister is Snorri the Priest, who alone of us has prospered; for though no slayings have ever happened in our branch, unlucky are we all, as is plain to see."

"I have often wondered," said Rolf, "how it is that we live here in this great hall and have but us three and the servants to fill it. There are places for seven fires down the middle of the hall, yet we use but one. And all the benches were once used, since they are worn: seats for fifty men, and the women's seats besides."

"Once," said Hiarandi, "my father had so many on his farm that nightly the hall was full. But those serving-men are Einar's now, and all our riches have passed away to him. Yet this house is the finest in all these parts. I was at the building of it in my youth, and" (here he was made sure that the thrall was not listening) "I myself made the secret panels by which we can escape in case of burning. For since that burning so long ago, no Soursop builds himself a house in which men may trap him."

"But thou hast no enemies, father?" asked the lad.

"No enemies, I hope," answered Hiarandi, "but few friends, I am sure, since only Frodi the Smith, my mother's cousin, is of our kin; for I count not Snorri the Priest."

"But why not Snorri the Priest?" asked Rolf.

"My father," answered Hiarandi, "quarrelled with him and called him coward. For Snorri would not take up at arms a suit my father lost at law."

Then Rolf thought a while. All men knew of Snorri the Priest, who was no temple priest at all but a priest of the law. For the title had come down from heathen times, when leaders had sway over all matters, both in religion and law, and to be priest was to be chieftain. But usage and the new religion changed that by degrees; so that to be priest now meant to be a giver of the law, with a seat at the Quarter Courts and at the Althing, the great yearly gathering to which from all Iceland men went to settle suits. And Snorri the Priest was well known as the richest man in Broadfirth dales, the shrewdest and wisest in all things worldly, and a master at the law.

"It would be well," said the lad, "to have Snorri on our side."

"It is better," said Asdis, "never to go to the law. Lawsuits and quarrels are bad things, and they bring a man's fortune to naught."

And Hiarandi added, "By law we have ever suffered."

Then Rolf was silent, and thought of what had been said: how the old woman had prophesied trouble at the law, and by what man that trouble should come. And as he thought upon the words she and his father had spoken, he thought that they had spoken with knowledge, though of different kinds: for while the woman prophesied vaguely, his father had seemed to know who the man should be.

"Father," asked Rolf, "knowest thou who the man is that came upon the ship?"

"I know," answered Hiarandi.

Asdis asked: "Who then is he?"

Hiarandi said: "Saw ye upon the ship, as it lay below us, the faces of any of the men?"

"Aye," answered they both, "for it was as clear as day."

"Saw ye then," asked Hiarandi, "one who stood by the mast, a tall man with a great beard?"

"I saw him," answered Rolf. "He stood and held by a rope and the mast, and I thought he should be the captain; but he gave no commands, nor did any man heed him, for all worked of themselves."

"Yet, as I guess," said Hiarandi, "the captain was he, and he was the man of whom the carline spoke."

"Who is he, then?" asked the boy.

"Listen," said Hiarandi, "and I will tell thee of one in my family of whom I have never yet spoken. There were two of us when I was a lad, brothers; and the other was named Kiartan. He was younger than I by a year, and different in all his ways; yet I have often thought that my father had not enough patience with him. For he sent him to bad companions rather than weaned him from them, and at last he drove him from the house altogether. Then Kiartan took to the sea—he was not bad, remember, but weak perhaps and foolish—took to the sea, and we saw him not for years. Once only he came back, out at elbow, and asked my father for money. Money he got, but gave the promise to ask nothing from the inheritance; and this was handselled before witnesses, my father giving much, the rest to come to me. Then Kiartan went away again, and not until this night have I seen him. But if that was his ship, then he has prospered."

"Yet it was he the woman meant?" asked Rolf.

"Who else?" returned his father.

"How should he," asked the boy, "bring trouble on thee?"

"I see not," answered Hiarandi, "how he should bring either evil or good."

Then he closed his mouth and became thoughtful, in a manner he had. Asdis motioned Rolf to be silent, and nothing more was said in the matter.

III

Kiartan at Cragness

ON THE MORNING of the fifth day thereafter, as Rolf stood by the gate of the enclosure which protected the farm buildings, he saw a man coming on a horse, and knew him for his father's brother Kiartan. He was a big man, heavily bearded, dressed in bright-colored clothes and hung about with gold chains. His eye was bright and roving; his face was genial, and he looked about him as he came as one who is well contented. Yet Rolf liked him not.

Now Kiartan rode up to the enclosure and saw the boy. "Ho!" he cried, "come hold my horse and stable him." So Rolf took the horse by the bridle and held him while the man dismounted. Then the boy started to lead the beast to the stable.

"Where is thy mistress?" asked Kiartan.

"My mother is in the house," answered Rolf.

"Now," Kiartan cried, "I took thee for a stable-boy. But thy father had ever a love of the earth, and so perhaps hast thou. Knowest thou me?"

"Thou art my uncle," replied the lad.

17

"Now," cried Kiartan, staring, "what spirit told thee of me?"

"Five nights ago," answered Rolf, "thou stoodst below on the deck of thy ship, and lookedst up at Cragness. And our beacon saved thee."

"Aye," said Kiartan. "We had work to save our lives, and a close miss we made of the Tusks." But he never gave a word of thanks, either to Rolf or to Hiarandi, for the saving of his life. "Thou art wise to stay at home, boy; for see how a sailor's life hangs ever on a thread. Now stable the horse, and I will see thy mother. The farmer is likely in the field."

So Rolf stabled the horse, and called his father from his work; and Hiarandi came, muttering (though he meant not that Rolf should hear), "Poor steel comes often home for a new edge." But he greeted his brother well, and bade him stay with them for the winter.

"Even for that am I come," answered Kiartan. "For my cargo is already sold, and my ship laid up for the winter near Hvamm, and I come home to my kinsman. No poor penny am I this time, to need any man's help. Perhaps," and he looked about him, "I can even help thee."

But the buildings were neat and weather-tight, and the farm was in no need of improvement. "I need nothing," said Hiarandi, "and I even have money out at call there in the neighborhood where thy ship is laid. But come, the wife prepares the meal. Lay aside thy cloak and be at home."

And so Kiartan entered on his wintering at Cragness.

Quiet is the winter in Iceland, when men have no work to do in the field, save the watching of horses and the feeding of the sheep and kine. Weather-wise must a man be to prepare against the storms, which sweep with suddenness from off the water and enfold the land with snow. Yet Hiarandi's flocks were small, and his sheep-range was not wide, and both he and Rolf were keen to see the changes in the weather; and as for their horses, they stayed ever near the buildings. So all were free to go to the gatherings which men made for games and ball-play, in times of fair weather. Thither Kiartan loved to go, dressed in his fine clothes, and talking much. But nights when he sat at home he would speak of his travels, and what a fine place the world was, and how little there was for a man here in Iceland. He said it was nothing to be a farmer, but a great thing to rove the sea, and to live, not in this land where all were equal, but where there were kings, earls, and other great men.

Once as he spoke thus he provoked Hiarandi to words. "Meseems, brother," the farmer said, "that thou hast forgotten the way our forefathers thought. For it was to avoid kings and earls that they left their lands in Norway and came over the sea hither. And those whom thou prizest so high are so little thought of here that we make nothing of them whatever."

"Now," answered Kiartan, "thy neighbor Einar

thinks well of earls, for he has fostered his son with the Earl of the Orkneys."

"The lad will understand little of our ways when he returns," replied Hiarandi.

"For all that," Kiartan said, "I name the son of Einar luckier than thy son here. A great court is held in the Orkneys, and all matters are to be learned there."

Then Hiarandi made response: "No court can teach good sense to a dolt, and no wisdom will flourish unless there be good ground for it to sprout. I have seen wise men bred in this little land, and fools that came out of Norway."

Then Kiartan talked not so much before Hiarandi of the things he had seen, nor for a time before Rolf either. But when there came again the great winter ball-play, to which all went, and Rolf shot again with the bow before them all, and proved himself the most skillful, though not yet the strongest: after that Kiartan made more of the lad.

"Men," he said to Rolf one day when they were alone, "may be able to shoot farther than thou with the bow, for two did it. But none shot so surely. And some day thou wilt outshoot them as well."

"I think not much of it," answered Rolf.

"Now," said Kiartan, "thou shouldst learn to prize thyself higher. For in the Orkneys good archers are welcome in the Earl's body-guard, and a man is honored and well paid."

"Yet he is no longer his own man," answered Rolf.

"What of that?" asked Kiartan. "If for a few years he can see the world, and make his fortune also, then he is forever after a greater man at home. Think more of thyself!"

And at other times he spoke in the same strain, bidding Rolf value himself higher. And he told of the great world, and described his journeys. For he had been, he said, as far as the the great Middle Sea, had traded in Italy, and had even seen Rome. And Rolf was greatly interested in those tales; for the lands across the sea were of moment to all Icelanders, since many a man fared abroad often, and no man thought himself complete who had not once made the voyage. So he listened willingly, when Kiartan told his tales at evening in the hall. The parents were inattentive; but sometimes Hiarandi, and sometimes Asdis, would interrupt the story, sending the lad to some task or to bed.

Now at last it draws toward spring, and the time approaches when Kiartan must go away to his ship, to dight it for the voyage. And it was remembered afterward how one evening he drew Hiarandi on to talk of his savings, and learned what money he had out at interest, and with whom. And Kiartan spoke the oftener with Rolf, praising him for the fine man he was growing to be. Then at his last night at Cragness the shipmaster said, as all sat together before the fire:

"Brother, thou knowest I must go away tomorrow."

"Aye," answered Hiarandi.

"Now," said Kiartan, "let me say to thee what is in my mind. Take it not ill that I speak freely. But I think it wrong of thee that thou keepest here at home such a fine lad as is Rolf thy son." And he would have put his hand upon the boy's shoulder, but Rolf drew away. Kiartan went on: "Now I am going to the South Isles. Send Rolf with me, and let him see the world."

Then Hiarandi grew uneasy, and he answered: "Speak no more of this. Some day he shall see the lands across the main, but as yet he is too young."

"Nay," answered Kiartan, "he is nearly full-grown. What sayest thou, Rolf? Wilt thou not go with me?"

Rolf answered: "I will be ruled by my father."

"I have made much money," reasoned Kiartan, "and thou canst do the same."

"I care not for trading," replied Rolf.

"There are courts to be seen," said Kiartan, "and thou mayest serve in them thyself."

"I am not ready to be a servant," quoth Rolf.

"But thou mayest see wars and fighting," cried Kiartan.

"I have no quarrels of my own," answered the boy, "and I mix not in the affairs of others."

Now Hiarandi and Asdis had listened with both anger and fear,—anger that Kiartan should so tempt the boy, and fear at what Rolf might answer. But Rolf spoke with wisdom beyond his years; and at his last response Hiarandi smiled, and Asdis clapped her hands. Then Kiartan started from his seat and cried:

"Out upon ye all for stay-at-homes!" And he would speak no more with them that night, but went to his locked bed and shut himself in. Yet he spoke to the lad once more in the morning, out by the byre while Rolf was saddling the horse.

"Surely," said Kiartan, "thou didst not mean what thou saidst last night, for the fear of thy parents was in thy mind. Now let me tell thee what we can do. I will go on for the lading of my ship, and that will take a fortnight's time. Then I will wait for thee at the mouth of Laxriver, and thou canst come thither and join me secretly."

"Now," said the lad, "if I tell my father this, he will give thee a beating. Therefore I will remain silent until thy ship has sailed."

Then Kiartan turned pale, and cursed, and made as if to strike his nephew. But Rolf put his hand to his belt, and Kiartan drew away. Yet Rolf had no knife.

"I see," said Rolf, "that thou art not quick at arms nor sure of thy own strength, even against me. And I knew thou wert a coward long ago, when I saw thee on thy ship's deck, giving no orders, but letting other men save thy ship and thyself. No great deeds of daring would I see with thee as shipmaster."

When Kiartan rode away, he was as glad at parting as were those of the house.

"He is not changed," said Hiarandi, "in all the years he has been gone."

"Where," asked Asdis, "is the harm which he was to do us?"

And she laughed, but rejoiced too soon. For after six weeks men came to Hiarandi, sent from Laxriverdale, where traders had given goods to Kiartan upon his promise that Hiarandi should pay. And it was discovered that Kiartan had not only used the money which Hiarandi had out at call in that region, but had obtained goods from other men creating debts. And he had filled all his ship at Hiarandi's expense. Then Rolf told to his father his own tale of Kiartan's secret offer, and Hiarandi was bitterly wroth.

And then began those troubles which Thurid had foreseen. For when Hiarandi refused to pay for the goods, but instead sought to regain his money from those who had supplied Kiartan, the matter was brought to the law. And first at the Quarter Thing, and then at the Althing, many small suits were disputed. But the end of the matter was, that Hiarandi was beaten by the skill of the lawyers; and he had to lose his money and pay more besides, and stood stripped of all which he had laid up against his age, or against that time when Rolf should need a start in life. And the farmer was greatly cast down, recalling the misfortunes of the Soursops, and how he himself had been always called the Unlucky. But Asdis and Rolf strove to keep him in good heart.

IV

Of Einar and Ondott

NOW THE TALE turns to speak of Einar and
his household, how they dwelt at Fellstead, upon
the low-lying land. Einar was a rich man, and he kept
a large household of many thralls and servants. And
for his pleasure, that he might seem the greater in the
eyes of his neighbors, he kept men who did no work,
but bore arms wheresoever they went; yet it had never
been known that Einar brought any matter to blood-
shed. He was not firm in any dealings, but he wished
to be thought a great man. His holding was wide, for
he owned all that the fathers of Hiarandi had had.
Yet from his yard he often looked with no contented
eye toward the hall of Hiarandi, where it stood above
the crags, looking far over firth and fell.

Now of the men of Einar's household Ondott had
the ruling, for he pleased Einar much, yet they were
different in all outward ways. For Einar was short and
plump, given to puffing and swelling as he spoke, and
of many smooth words; but Ondott was tall and thin,
lean-visaged and sour, and of surly speech. Einar was
fond of dress, while Ondott went in simple clothes;

yet they both loved money, and some accused Ondott of hoarding, but Einar spent freely, seeking to gain by gifts what his wit could not win for him. For he was not loved, and men thought little of his counsels.

Of the women at Fellstead one old freedwoman was chief; and she held in especial care the daughter of Einar, Helga by name, who was yet young, being but thirteen years of age. She was of a sweet nature. Now one morning Helga stood with Dalla the old woman before the women's door of the hall, and they saw where came toward them a woman much bent, and covered with a cape and hood; when she came near, they knew her for Thurid from Cragness. She begged them for lodging and work. Dalla sent for Einar.

"How is it come," asked Einar, "that thou hast left Hiarandi?"

"The man," said she, "calls upon his doom, and I will not stay to share it." And she told of the beacon, and how thereby a ship had been saved.

"Now," quoth Einar, "Hiarandi is a fool, so to break an old custom."

"Yet meseems," said Helga timidly, "that it was a kind thing to do."

"Thou art but a child," he answered reprovingly. But she came closer to him and pulled his sleeve.

"Let not the old woman stay here," she whispered. "For I like not her looks, and I mistrust her."

But Ondott, who heard, said: "Nay, let us keep the old carline, if only to spite Hiarandi." And Dalla added: "She is a good worker, and handy to have about the place. Let us give her room." So Einar bade Thurid go within, and do what work was set her, in pay for her keep. But he asked her before he went away:

"Why camest thou here?"

"A rat," said she, "will leave a house that is sure to fall, and seek one which will stand." Then Einar was greatly pleased with her, and bade give her a better cloak. So it was that Thurid dwelt at Fellstead, and paid well with her work for her keep; but at Cragness she was missed, and the work was harder. Yet Thurid made no more prophecies, nor spoke of those which had been made. But it was known that the thralls of Hiarandi were set to light beacons on stormy nights, and he was much laughed at by the dwellers at Fellstead. And his thralls found it hard work, and became greatly discontented; yet since it was winter time, they had little else to do.

Now one of them was named Malcolm, a Scot, and he came one day to Fellstead, when he was not needed at the farm. And Ondott met him, and asked him in, and asked him questions of matters at Cragness. As they spoke by the fire, Thurid passed by, and she sang to herself:

> "Evil and ill
> Come together still."

Malcolm asked: "Does the woman still make her rhymes with you?"

"Little have I heard her sing," answered Ondott. "But what sang she with you?"

Then Malcolm told of the singing of Thurid and Asdis, and of the prophecies of the old woman. And when he went away, Ondott gave him a small piece of money and bade him come again. Then Ondott called Thurid, and asked her of the things she had said at Cragness, what they might mean. But he got little from her; for first she would not speak, and then she only muttered, and at last all she said was this rhyme:

"No need to teach
Or trick or speech
To him whose mind
All wiles will find."

And Ondott could make nothing out of that; moreover, because it was Kiartan whom Hiarandi had saved, he thought that the farmer had strengthened himself by his deed. For only when the news came of the trick of Kiartan in cheating his brother did Ondott think that there might be something in the old woman's forecasting. And he and Einar spoke cheerfully together of the misfortune to their neighbor. Then summer drew on, and the Quarter Thing was held, and then came bad news to Einar in his hall.

For a seafaring man landed at Hunafloi, and came across to Broadfirth; and he brought word that in the Orkneys Kiartan had foully slain a man of Broadfirth, whose nearest of kin was Einar, so that it was Einar's duty to follow up the blood-suit.

Here it must be said, for those who know not the customs of those days, that the death of a man called for atonement from the slayer, either his death or a payment in money, unless the slaying could be justified. The nearest of kin must take the suit against the slayer; and if the slayer should die, then his nearest of kin must take the defence. And the law is clearly shown by the case of the Heath-Slayings and other famous quarrels, when from small broils great feuds arose, from the duty of kinship and the unwillingness to pay blood-fines for another's deed. Thus Einar took upon him his duty, and vowed that Kiartan should pay with either money or blood.

All stood by and heard this, and they applauded. But Ondott said: "Come now outside with me and speak of this, but give the messenger food and bid him rest here the night."

So that was done, and Einar went out into the yard with Ondott, and walked up and down with him. Said Ondott:

"Long have we likely to wait ere we lay hands on Kiartan. For he hath set his own brother strong against him, and scarce will he dare return to Iceland."

"That may be true," said Einar gloomily.

"I like it not," said Ondott, "that Hiarandi should know this spite his bother has done thee, and yet be free himself. In the old days, which are not so long past, a man would have gone against Hiarandi with weapons. And he hath no relatives to harm thee."

"For all that," answered Einar, "the men of the Quarter would not like it. Lawfully must vengeance be taken, or not at all. Yet it is hard if my money and thy wit cannot rid me of these brothers, who anger me, and Hiarandi more than Kiartan." And he looked across at Cragness with fretting.

"Well mayest thou say that," answered Ondott, "for there stands Hiarandi's hall, which he cannot fill, while thou in thine art cramped for room. It is plainly true what people say, that thou canst never come into the honor which should be thine, while thou lives here, where strangers take thee for Hiarandi's tenant, or even his freeman."

"They take me for his freeman!" cried Einar. "Now that is not to be borne! And I say to thee, get me Hiarandi's house and I will reward thee well."

Then Ondott laid a plan before him. It should be given out that Kiartan was dead: the man who brought the news of the slaying might be bribed to swear to Kiartan's death. Then the blood-suit could be brought against Hiarandi in place of Kiartan; and all men knew that Hiarandi had no money to pay the fine, so that he must sell his farm.

"Now," quoth Einar in great delight, "I will lengthen thy name, and thou shalt be called Ondott Crafty." For that was a saying in those days, to lengthen a man's name by giving him a nickname.

Then they called from the house that man who had brought the news. Because he was an outlander he was easily persuaded to swear to Kiartan's death. Einar gave him money, both for himself and to pay his passage outward. Then witnesses were called to hear the oath; and on the morrow the man departed, and took ship for Ireland, and he is out of the story.

V

The Summoning of Hiarandi

WHEN THAT MAN who brought the news and made the false swearing was well out of the country, then Ondott bestirred himself to go against Hiarandi. Said he to Einar:

"It is time that we summon Hiarandi soon to answer to the blood-suit, for the sitting of the Althing draws nigh."

To that Einar assented, and on the morrow Ondott bade two men arm themselves and go with them to Cragness.

"Why need we men?" asked Einar.

"We must have witnesses to the summoning," answered Ondott.

"But it is not necessary to bear arms," said Einar.

"We will prepare ourselves," replied Ondott, "as becomes thy dignity and as regards thy safety, for Hiarandi hath a quick temper." Then Einar said no more, and they rode to Cragness. But Ondott knew well that at such summonings quarrels often arose; and he said privily to his men, Hallmund and Hallvard:

"Look that your swords be loose in their sheaths."

They rode into the yard at Cragness and called Hiarandi from his house. Hiarandi came, and with him Rolf, bearing his bow, for he was about to go out for birds.

"Hiarandi," said Einar, "we have come to speak of the blood-suit for the slaying of my kinsman."

"That thy kinsman is slain I knew," answered Hiarandi, "but I see not how it affects me in any way, so long as my brother be living."

"But thy brother is dead," replied Einar, and told that Kiartan was ship-wrecked in the Orkneys.

"This is the first I have heard of it," said Hiarandi.

Then Ondott spoke. "Knowing thy suspicious nature," said he, "I brought with us the men who were witnesses to the oath the messenger made. Thus canst thou know thy brother is truly dead."

Hallvard and Hallmund said they had witnessed the oath. Hiarandi answered no word, but looked from one to the other.

"Now," said Ondott, "these same men will be witnesses to what we say here together." And this he said in a manner to provoke Hiarandi, yet he still answered nothing.

"Is it not better," asked Einar, "that this matter be settled here quietly, between neighbors, rather than be brought before the judges at the Althing?"

"Quietly settled is always best," answered Hiarandi. "Yet I see not how this matter is to be settled at all, seeing I have no money to make atonement."

"Now," said Ondott quickly to Einar, "let me speak for thee in this affair." Then Einar gave the matter into the hands of Ondott.

"All men know," began Ondott then, "that thou art poor, Hiarandi." And he saw Hiarandi flush with anger. Then he went on to propose that an exchange be made of Cragness for some parts of Einar's land, much less in value. And he spoke with such words that Hiarandi would feel insulted, and marked him grow ever redder in the face. When he had finished, Hiarandi burst out upon him.

"Foolish are ye to suppose," cried Hiarandi, "that I will ever give up this stead which my fathers have settled. Let this matter come to the courts of law."

Ondott spoke to Einar. "There is no reasoning with a madman. Thou must recite the summons."

Then Einar, who knew the law well, spoke the summons, and named the deed which was done on his kinsman, and made Hiarandi answerable; and called him to appear before the Quarter Court at the Althing, there to justify the slaying, or pay the blood-fine, or be made an outlaw. Everything he said in due legal form, and Ondott and the two men were named as witnesses.

Then he prepared to ride away, but Ondott spoke once more. "If thou canst not keep land, Hiarandi, better than thy father, then must thou lose this place in the end."

Hiarandi could not restrain his wrath. He spoke no word; but he strode to Ondott, and smote him with his staff. Ondott warded the blow, but the arm was broken at the wrist.

Then Ondott cried to Hallvard and Hallmund: "Set upon him!" Those two drew their swords, and in that moment Hiarandi stood in danger of his life. But Rolf had strung his bow and set an arrow on the string. He drew the shaft to its head, and aimed at Einar, and cried: "Now Einar dies if my father is hurt!"

They drew away hastily, and dared do no more, for they knew the aim of the lad. Nothing more was done in violence; yet before he rode away did Ondott summon Hiarandi for that hurt to him. And there the matter rested, with two suits against Hiarandi. Then all was quiet until the time came for folk to ride to the Althing.

VI

Of What Hiarandi Should Do

HIARANDI SPOKE not at all of the suits against him, yet he was continually gloomy. And one day he said:

"Much better were it now, had I never lighted the beacon that night."

"Thou knowest," responded Asdis, "that thou didst right."

"Still," said Hiarandi, "summer gales oft bring wrecks, and one ship might pay the blood-fine for me."

"For all that," Asdis answered, "thou hast not now the heart to stop lighting the beacon."

Then on the second night thereafter came a storm; but nothing was said, except that Hiarandi bade the beacon be lighted. Yet he was gloomier than ever.

One night Rolf asked him: "Why is it that thou art to answer for that deed which my uncle has done?"

"One must answer for a kinsman's deed," answered his father, "when that kinsman is dead."

"And what is the punishment," asked Rolf, "for slaying?"

"A fine or outlawry," replied Hiarandi. "Tell me of outlawry," begged Rolf. "For I hear of outlaws who live and work among men, and of those who flee into hiding, and of those who go overseas." "There are outlaws of many kinds," answered Hiarandi. "Some outlaws are condemned not to leave a district, or even a farm; but some must leave Iceland or else defend their lives. But most outlawries are like this, that a man must go abroad three winters, and then he is free to return. If he stays, his enemies may slay him if they can, and no man may ask atonement. Thus they who burned Njal in his house did fare abroad; but on the other hand Gisli our ancestor lived in hiding, and would not go. And Grettir the Strong, as all men know, lives to-day an outlaw, in one district or another; and no man has taken him, though there is a great price set upon his head."

"If thou art made outlaw," asked Rolf, "what wilt thou do?"

"Ask me not," said Hiarandi. "For the matter troubles me. If I go abroad, how will ye all live? And it will profit you nothing if I stay and am slain. Yet if I am made outlaw, and go not, my goods and the farm are forfeit."

As greatly as Hiarandi feared the outcome of these suits, so were those at Fellstead pleased by their hopes. And no one heard the carline Thurid, who sang to herself when she heard Ondott boast:

"He laughs too soon
Who doth forget,
Soursop blood
Binds kinsmen yet."

But Asdis thought rightly in the matter. For she said to Hiarandi: "What wilt thou do for thy defence at law? Is there no lawyer to help thee?"

"Help is offered," answered her husband, "to those who have money. And I have none."

"Then wilt thou ask help of Snorri the Priest? There is no other to give thee counsel."

"Not close," replied Hiarandi, "is the tie of blood between us, and small is the friendship. Moreover, Snorri draws ever to those who wax in fortune, and such is Einar; and he helps little those whose fortunes wane, and such am I."

"Now," cried Asdis, "be not as a man who sees his own doom, and stirs not to help himself. Where is thy manhood? Bestir thyself for my sake and Rolf's, and do what thou canst for our good! Now promise me that thou wilt ask help of Snorri."

Thus she stirred Hiarandi to shake off his gloom, so that he promised. And when the time came for him to ride to the Althing, he went with a better heart.

VII

How Hiarandi Received the Lesser Outlawry

HIARANDI TRAVELLED to the Althing all alone; he had a good horse and stout clothes, but in nothing was he noticeable, so that men who passed him on the road gave him only the good-day, yet asked him not to join their company. And he saw how men of power rode with their Thingmen behind them, all in colored clothes and well armed. He saw Hrut, the famous swordsman, how he rode with eleven full-grown sons at his back, and men besides, so that all thought that a grand sight. And many others rode to the Althing with great pride. Then Hiarandi recalled that his own father had ridden in holiday guise to bring his suits; and as he compared his father's state with his own, he who went alone and unnoticed, but at home was called the Unlucky, then his heart was greatly cast down within him.

He came to the Thingvalla, where all the plain was a busy hive of men. And he found humble lodging at a booth, and stabled his horse under the cliff, and spent the night alone amid the throng. Then on the morrow, at midday, he went out to have speech with Snorri. At Snorri's booth he was told that Snorri was at talk with a client within.

"Then I will wait," said Hiarandi, and sat down on a bench at the door. But it was bitter to him that he should sit there, a poor suitor, at the door of his kinsman.

Now he had not sat there long when he heard his own name spoken within, and he knew the voice of his neighbor Einar. And Einar was saying, "Thou are not bound to Hiarandi in any way."

Then he heard another voice, the voice of an old man—for Snorri was advanced in years—saying: "Small enough are the ties between myself and Hiarandi."

Then Hiarandi rose and walked away. And he forgot all he had promised his wife, and all she had said to him: how he should forget himself in struggling for her sake and Rolf's. But that melancholy came over him which was his greatest weakness.

"I am too late," he said to himself, "for Einar is before me. My case is lost, and my farm too; for on whose side Snorri is, on that side has fallen the judgment for this score of years. And the twists of the law are too hard for me to understand, since meseems right hath no place in a law-finding. Yet I will defend myself as I may."

Then on the morrow the Althing was opened, and

the four Quarter Courts sat in their places, and the Fifth Court sat at the Hill of Laws. And Hiarandi, as he went to the court of the Westfirthers, saw where Einar walked also thither with Snorri, keeping close by his elbow, and laughing as he talked. Ondott also was there, slinking behind like a fox. And on that very first day Hiarandi's case was called early.

Now Einar had men of the law as his friends, and they had taught him what to say. And he opened the case, speaking loud and clearly, and called on Hiarandi to answer the charges. But Hiarandi stood up alone, without counsel, and spoke for himself. Soon he saw that the case went against him. For Einar and his friends knew so much of the law that their wiles were many, and Hiarandi was soon confused, so that his answers were not wise. And Einar smiled where he stood, so that he confused Hiarandi the more. Then Einar demanded judgment unless Hiarandi had more to say. And he was about to give up his case.

Then came some one and stood at Hiarandi's elbow, and said: "Thou shouldst demand a stay in the proceedings."

Hiarandi looked at the man, but he was muffled in a cloak, so that his face was not to be seen. Then Hiarandi asked: "For what reason can I ask a stay?"

The man replied: "It is always permitted to ask it, to get counsel."

But Hiarandi said: "No counsel can save me here. Let an end come now."

"Foolish art thou," answered the man. "Dost thou forget those at home? Do as I bid!"

Then Hiarandi asked a stay, and it was granted him until the morrow. But when he turned to ask the man his advice, he was gone, and Hiarandi could not see him anywhere. Then he went to beg help of those versed in the law, but they said he should have come sooner, for they were now too busy to help him. Once more, thinking again of Asdis and Rolf, he went to ask help of Snorri the Priest; but he was not at his booth, and men said he would be at the courts all day. At that Hiarandi went away again; and he wandered about the Thingfield, seeing no one whom he could ask for help, but beholding everywhere men too busy with their own affairs to heed him. At last towards dusk his courage forsook him once more, and he went and sat down on the bank of the river, believing his case lost. As he sat there the light grew dim, and of a sudden he saw at his side the man muffled in the cloak.

"Now is seen," said the man, "the truth of the old saw: 'He that pleadeth his own cause hath a fool for his client.' For a sound case hadst thou, but it is well-nigh ruined beyond remedy."

"What should I have done?" asked Hiarandi.

"Thou shouldst have asked aid of Snorri the Priest."

"But he," said Hiarandi, "has been in talk with Einar, who sues me."

"Since when," asked the man, "has Snorri been

used to pledge himself to all who come to him? Hast thou forgotten he is of thy kin?"

"We are both come," said Hiarandi, "from the stock of Gisli the Outlaw. But if Gisli was his uncle, so also was Gisli the slayer of his father. So Snorri is both against us and for us by the tie of blood; and he forgetteth and remembereth as he chooseth, or as his interest bids."

Then said the man: "Thou givest him no good character. Yet at least thou couldst have let him have the say, which way his interest lies."

But Hiarandi answered in bitter mood: "Snorri casteth his weight where is the greater power, that his own strength may grow."

"He would not thank thee should he hear thee," answered the stranger. "Yet methinks that even in matters which concern his own advancement, he should be free to choose for himself."

"Now," asked Hiarandi, "shall I go to Snorri and crave his help?"

"Nay," replied the cowled man, "now it is too late. For this evening Snorri holdeth counsel on weighty matters concerning chiefs from the south firths, who are to meet him at his booth."

"Why, then," asked Hiarandi, "didst thou persuade me to ask a stay of judgment? For my fate meets me after all."

"Perhaps even I," said the man, "know more of the law than thou. Now wilt thou be ruled by me?"

"That I will," answered Hiarandi quickly.

"Then shalt thou do thus and so," said the man. And he instructed Hiarandi how he should speak on the next day. "And this shalt thou do even though thou seest Snorri in company with Einar. —Nay, make no question, for else thou art ruined." And with this the man went away.

In the morning all men go to the courts again; and Hiarandi marks how Einar walks with Snorri, and they seem merry together, though Einar laughs the most. Nevertheless, Hiarandi stands up when his case is called, and does as the cowled man had said, for he demands of Einar what forfeiture he will name.

"Either," said Einar, "that thou shalt pay down the worth of three hundreds in silver, or that thou shalt be outlawed."

"Now," said Hiarandi, "it seems hard that so much shall be my punishment. But wilt thou take this offer, that we handsel this case to Snorri the Priest, and abide by his finding?"

Einar hesitated. But many standing by said that was fair; moreover, that was a custom much followed. And again, Einar did not wish the outlawing of Hiarandi; but he felt sure that Snorri would lay a blood-fine, which must force Hiarandi to sell his farm. And he thought his cause was sure, so he said after a moment:

"I will."

So they handselled the suit to Snorri, striking hands together before the judges, and agreeing to abide by his decision. Then Snorri stood up to speak. Einar smiled at him that he might remind him of their companionship, but Snorri smiled not at all.

"Thus it seems to me," he said, and all men listened while he spoke—for Snorri was one of those who had known the great men of old time, who had seen the great fight at the Althing after Njal's Burning, and who had swayed its event. "Thus it seems to me," said Snorri. "The case of Hiarandi was a good one at the beginning, yet he has well-nigh spoiled it. But the case of Einar seems strong, yet it is weak. For he has named as witnesses two men of kin to the slain man; also he has not called a man who is nearer neighbor than one he has called. Also these men are neither landholders, nor money owners, nor owners of sheep or cattle; but they live in Einar's hall at his expense. Now let Einar say if all these things are not true."

Then Einar had to speak; and he acknowledged that his witnesses, who should make the jury, were chosen as Snorri had said. Then Snorri set those men out of the jury, and only six were left.

"Seven men are needed to make the tale of the witnesses complete," quoth Snorri. "Therefore it is plain that this case of the slaying shall fall to the ground, and no atonement shall be paid. But as to the case of the striking of Ondott, that is another matter; and it is a case of contempt of the Thing, for one who goes to serve summons in a suit is free to go and come unscathed, and is under the protection of the men of the Quarter. Therefore I doom Hiarandi to the lesser outlawry, after this manner: he shall remain upon his farm for the space of one year, nor go beyond its limits more than the length of a bow-shot, upon penalty of full outlawing. But shall he become a full outlaw, then his property, and the inheritance of his son, is not to be forfeit, but only Hiarandi's life is to be in danger. And such is my finding." Then Snorri sat him down.

Then men murmured together, discussing the judgment; and all said that he knew the law to its uttermost quibble, and he knew men as well, for who told him that the jury was wrongly constituted?

And Einar was wroth, complaining that Snorri was tender of his relative. But Hiarandi was glad, and a weight fell from him, for he saw how he had been saved from all that threatened him. He went to Snorri to thank him.

Snorri took his thanks, and smiled at Hiarandi. "Now is clearly seen," quoth he, "how much Snorri thinks of his own honor, and how little of that of his kinsmen."

Hiarandi had nothing to answer.

"And it is also plain," said Snorri, "how I always favor the rich, but care nothing for poor men."

"Now I see," said Hiarandi, "that thou wert the man in the cloak."

"Mayest thou perceive as well," responded Snorri, "that thou hast a friend in the world who will help thee when he can." But he would take no more thanks, advising Hiarandi to go home and set his affairs in order, since from the rising of the Althing to its next sitting he must not quit his farm.

"And take heed," quoth Snorri, "that thou losest not thy life from carelessness, or from the wiles of thine enemies."

Then Hiarandi betook himself home.

VIII

Of Schemings

UNTIL THE TIME when the Althing must rise, Hiarandi set his affairs in order, and was busy thereat. He arranged who should buy his hay, and who should supply him with this matter and that, although it was clear that many things must be done by the hands of Rolf. Also Frodi the Smith, kinsman of the Cragness-dwellers, was to come to Cragness whenever he might. Thus it was all settled; and when the Althing rose, then Hiarandi withdrew upon his farm for the space of one year.

But Rolf had to see to the sheep-shearing, since the washing was best done beyond the farm, upon common land. Also the selling of the wool came to Rolf's lot, and he travelled to the market therewith. Through the autumn he was much busied with his father's matters; and it rejoiced his parents that the lad, who had come now into his fifteenth year, was wise and foreseeing, and looked well to all that was trusted to his hand. Then the winter drew nigh; and the hay was stored, and the time came when the sheep must be gathered from their summer pastures, when the frost drove them down from the uplands. All men met at the great sheep-fold which the father of Hiarandi had built; but Hiarandi might not be there, because the fold was now on Einar's land, full five bowshots from the boundaries of Cragness. Rolf went with the thralls to the separating of the sheep by means of their marks; but Hiarandi sat at home, looking out at the gathering of people, and might not be at any of the doings.

Now Ondott Crafty had oversight of Einar's sheep, and he examined the sheep's ear-marks, and said whose they were. Rolf gave to the thralls the sheep to drive home; but Frodi the Smith, who was the mildest of men, took the sheep from the hands of Ondott. This task Rolf gave to Frodi, because he would not himself have speech with Ondott, who was now well of his broken arm, but whose temper was not improved by his hurt. Now Ondott came to a sheep which had torn its ear, so that the mark was scarred. Then said Ondott:

"This sheep is Einar's."

"Nay," said Frodi, "I remember the wether, and he is Hiarandi's."

"Looks not the mark," asked Ondott, "like the mark of Einar?"

"Yes," said Frodi, "but the mark is scarred, and is changed."

"Now," quoth Ondott, "call Hiarandi hither, and let him decide."

This he said with a sneer; but Frodi answered

gravely: "My cousin shall not break his outlawry for a sheep. But call Rolf hither."

"I call no boys to my counsel," answered Ondott. "The matter is between thee and me."

Then Frodi was perplexed, for in disputes and bargains he mixed little. "But," said he, "meseems this is best. Drive the sheep to Cragness, and let Hiarandi see it."

"Now," said Ondott, "I have no time for that. But draw thy whittle, and we can settle the matter here."

Then Frodi looked upon his long knife, and said nothing.

"Why carriest thou the whittle, then," asked Ondott, "if thou art not ready to use it?"

"My whittle," answered Frodi, "is to cut my bread and cheese, and to mend my shoes on a journey."

Then all the men who stood about hooted at the simple answer. Ondott said: "Betake thyself then to bread and cheese, but the sheep is ours." And he sent the sheep away to join Einar's flock.

Now Frodi was puzzled, and he said: "I will not follow up the matter, but will pay for the sheep out of mine own savings."

But when he offered to pay, Rolf and Hiarandi were angered, for the wether was a good one. Yet they could get no satisfaction from Einar, although they might not blame Frodi, knowing his peaceful nature.

Now, as the winter approached, came chapmen, traders, into the neighborhood, and laid up their ship near Cragness; and all men went to chaffer with them. But Hiarandi must stay at home. Then for company's sake he sent and bade the shipmaster dwell with him for the winter; but Ondott Crafty, learning of it, won the shipmaster, by gifts, to stay with Einar. And that pleased Hiarandi not at all. Then the winter came, and men had little to do, so they held ball-play on the ponds; yet Hiarandi could not go thither. And the life began to irk him much. When spring drew near, Frodi went back to his smithy, and the household was small.

One day Ondott said to Einar: "Still we sit here, and gaze at the house where we should live."

"What is there to do?" asked Einar. "Nothing brings Hiarandi from his farm, not even the loss of his wether. I have set spies to watch him, but he never comes beyond the brook which marks his boundary."

"Yet there is something to be done," answered Ondott. "Wait a while."

And the winter passed, and the chapmen began to dight their ship for the outward voyage. Now Malcolm the Scot, the thrall of Hiarandi, stood often on the crag when his day's work was done, and gazed at the ship of the chapmen. One evening Ondott went thither to him, seeing that he was out of sight of the hall.

"Why gazest thou," asked Ondott, "so much at the ship? Wouldst thou go in her?"

"Aye," answered the thrall, "for she goes to my

home. But I have not the money to purchase my freedom, though Hiarandi has promised in another year to set me free."

"Wilt thou wait another year when thou mightest slip away now?" cried Ondott. "But perhaps thou fearest that the shipmaster would give thee up."

"That also," said the thrall, "was in my mind."

Then Ondott said: "The shipmaster has dwelt with us the winter through, and I know well what sort of man he is. Now I promise that if thou comest to him three nights hence, he will keep thee hidden, and no one shall see thee when they sail in the morning."

The thrall hesitated, but in the end he did as Ondott desired, and he gained his freedom by the trick. Thus was the work at Cragness rendered harder for those who remained, and Frodi could not come to help.

"Hiarandi," said Ondott to Einar, "is at last coming into those straits where I wished him. Now be thou guided by me, and I promise that in the end thy wishes will be fulfilled. Come, we will go to Cragness as before, and make offer to Hiarandi to buy his land." And he persuaded Einar to go. They went as before, with Hallvard and Hallmund.

"Shall we go armed?" asked the men.

"Nay," answered Ondott, "only witnesses do I desire."

Now when Hiarandi was called forth by Einar, Rolf also was by, but he saw that they of Fellstead bore no arms. Again Ondott spoke in the place of Einar.

"Hiarandi," said he, "all men can see what fortune is thine, since thy thrall has left thee and thy work is harder. Truly thou art called unlucky. But Einar pities thy condition, and he offers thus: Take from him a smaller farm, and the difference in silver. And since this outlawry is from us, from the time ye two handsel the bargain thou art free to go where thou wilt, without fear of thy life."

But Hiarandi spoke to Einar, and not to Ondott.

"Why comest thou hither," he said, "like a small man to chaffer over little things? This outlawry irks me not, and in two months I am free to go where I wish. Go home; and when thou comest again, find thy tongue and speak for thyself!"

Then he went indoors and left them.

So Einar and those others rode homeward, and he thought his journey shameful. "See," said he to Ondott, "where thy counsels have brought me. I am mocked and sent away."

"Now," Ondott replied, "that has happened which I desired, and I brought men to hear. For thou hast made a fair offer to Hiarandi, and hast shown a good heart. Now what happens to him is his own fault, and no man can blame us." Then he commanded the two men that they should tell everyone what had been said, showing how Einar had been generous, but Hiarandi insulting. And when

they reached the house, Ondott said to Einar in
private:

"Thou shalt see that Hiarandi hath sown the seeds
of his own destruction. Leave all to me."

Not many evenings thereafter, Ondott put himself
in the way of the second thrall of Hiarandi, and
spoke with him. "How goes all at Cragness?" asked
Ondott.

"Hard," said the thrall, "for we are at the spring
work; and Hiarandi spares not himself, nor me either,
and the work is heavy since my fellow is gone."

"Now, why not make thy lot lighter," asked Ondott, "by taking service elsewhere?"

"I am a slave," said the man, "and not a servant."
He did not tell that his freedom had been promised
him, for he thought that time far away, since it was
three years. For Hiarandi had the custom that a thrall
should serve with him not for life, but for only seven
years, and this man had been with him a less time
than Malcolm.

"The life of a thrall," said Ondott, "is very hard."

"Aye," said the man.

"Yet thy fellow went away," quoth Ondott.

"Aye," answered the thrall, "but he fled over the
sea. No ship is now outward bound, nor is there
anyone to hide me. Else might I also flee."

"Come to Einar," said Ondott. "There shalt thou
be safe."

"If thou sayest true," answered the thrall, "then it
shall be done."

"But thou must come," said Ondott, "in the way I shall name. Thus only shalt thou be of service to Einar; but thou shalt be well rewarded if thou showest thyself a man of courage."

"Who will not dare much for his freedom?" replied the thrall. "But is harm meant to Hiarandi?"

"That is not thine affair," quoth Ondott. Then for a time they spoke together, and certain matters were agreed upon between them.

IX

Of the Outcome of Ondott's Plottings

NOW SPRING WAS well advanced, but the work was ever hard at Cragness, and Hiarandi grew very weary. So his melancholy gained on him again. There came a morning when he was troubled in his demeanor, and spoke little. "What ails thee this day?" asked Asdis of him.

"Now," said Hiarandi, "for all my words to Einar, this life irks terribly. Better to be an outlaw, and go where I will—as doth Grettir the Strong, who lives secure from all his foes."

Asdis answered: "And what use then couldst thou be to thy wife and son; and is not the time short enough until the ban leaves thee? Be a man, and wait with patience a little while yet!"

"Yet something weighs upon me," pursued Hiarandi, "for last night I dreamed, and the dream forebodes ill. Methought I was working in the field, and I left my work and my land; some good reason I had, but it is not clear to me now. I did not go a bow-shot beyond the boundary, but from behind a copse wolves sprang out and fell upon me. As they tore me and I struggled, I awoke, yet the fear is heavy on me still."

Asdis laughed, though with effort, and quoth she: "Now take thy boat and fish near the rocks this day. Then no wolves can come near thee."

"Nay," answered Hiarandi, "How canst thou ask me to fish when so much must be done on the farm?"

"At least," said Asdis, "work on the northern slope, at the ploughing, and away from the boundary."

"The frost still lies there in the earth in places," replied Hiarandi. "But on the south slope, where the sun lies, all is ploughed and today we must seed."

"Take thy sword, then," begged Asdis, "and have it at thy side as thou workest. Then no wolf will hurt thee."

But Hiarandi answered, "The day is fine and the wind soft. The sun and the air will clear my head, and we will laugh at this at even-tide. I will take no sword, for it gets in the way."

Then he called the thrall and Rolf; and they took the bags of seed, and went out to work. Now that was a fine spring day, so fine that the like of it seldom comes. Old farmers in Broadfirth still call such a day a day of Hiarandi's weather.

But Asdis detained Rolf, and spoke to him earnestly. "Dreams often come true, and wolves in dreams mean death. See, I will lay by the door thy father's sword and thy bow, so that thou canst snatch them at need. Be near thy father this day, for I fear he is 'fey' (as is said of those who see their fate and avoid it not), and watch well what happens."

So Rolf stayed near his father all that morning, working with him and the thrall at the sowing. But nothing happened; and the sun and the air cleared from Rolf's head all fear of ill. Yet Hiarandi was still gloomy and absent-minded. Then when they stopped for their meal at noon, and ate it as they sat together on a rock, Rolf spoke to Hiarandi, trying to take his mind from himself.

"Tell me," he begged, "what sort of man is that outlaw Grettir the Strong, and for what is he outlawed?"

Then Hiarandi told the tale, and as he spoke he grew more cheerful. "Grettir," said he, "is the strongest man that ever lived in Iceland, and no three men can master him. For he himself hath said that he hath no fear of three, nor would he flee from four; but with five he would not fight unless he must. All his life he has been rough, impatient of control, and at home only amid struggles and slayings. Yet for all that he is a man of ill luck rather than misdeeds, for he hath been greatly hated and provoked. And it is great harm for Iceland that Grettir ever was outlawed. Now this was the cause of his outlawing. Once in Norway Grettir lay stormbound with his companions, and they had much ado to make the land at all. They lay under the lee of a dyke, and had no shelter nor wherewith to make fire, and the weather was exceeding cold, for winter was nigh. Then night came on, and they feared they should all freeze; and when they saw lights on the mainland across the sound, they desired greatly to unmoor their ship and cross, but dared not for the storm. Then Grettir, to save the lives of the others, swam the sound, and came to the hall where those lights were, and therein people were feasting. Then he went into the hall; but so huge is he, and so covered with ice were his clothes and hair and beard, that those in the hall thought him a troll. Up they sprang and set upon him, and some snatched firebrands to attack him, for no weapons will bite on witch or troll. He took a brand and warded himself, and won his way out, but not before fire had sprung from the brands to the straw in the hall. And he swam back with his brand to his companions, but the hall burned up, and all those that were therein. Now there were burned the sons of a man powerful here in Iceland; and for that deed, before ever he returned, Grettir was made outlaw. Because of the injustice he would not go away for his three years, but stayed here. Nigh sixteen years he has been outlaw now, and lives where he may, so that many rue his outlawry. And he is not to be overcome by either force or guile; great deeds, moreover, he has done in laying ghosts that walked, and monsters that preyed on men."

Now so far had Hiarandi got in his story, when he turned to the thrall who sat thereby. "At what lookest thou, man?"

"Nothing," answered the thrall, and turned his face another way.

"Methought thou wert looking, and signalling with the hand," said Hiarandi. "And is there something there in those willows on Einar's land? What didst thou see?"

"Nothing," answered the thrall again.

"Nevertheless," said Hiarandi, "go, Rolf, and fetch me my sword; for I repent that I came without weapon hither."

Now Rolf had seen nothing in the bushes; yet he went for the sword, and hastened, but the distance was two furlongs. Then after a while Hiarandi grew weary of waiting, and he saw nothing at all in the willows, so he said to the thrall: "Now let us go again to work."

But they had not worked long when the thrall looked privily, and he saw a hand wave in the willows. Then he cried aloud: "Good-by, master," and he ran toward the place. Hiarandi sprang from his work, and ran after the thrall.

Now the land at that place lay thus. At the foot of the slope was that brook which was Hiarandi's boundary, and toward the sea on Einar's land was the thicket of dwarf willows. And a gnarled oak grew at a place away from the willows, standing alone by itself.

So when Rolf came from the hall, bearing the sword, and having also his bow and arrows, he saw the thrall fleeing, and Hiarandi running after. They reached the brook, and leaped it, and ran on, Hiarandi pursuing most eagerly. The thrall ran well, but

Hiarandi used thought; for he turned a little toward the clump of willows, and cut the thrall off from them, where he might have hidden. Yet he might not catch the man, who fled past the oak. Then Hiarandi heard the voice of Rolf, calling him to stop; so he remembered himself, and stood still there at the oak, and turned back to go home. But men with drawn swords started up out of the willows, and ran at Hiarandi. He leaped to the tree, and set his back against it to defend himself. And Rolf, as he came running, saw how the men fell upon his father. The lad strung his bow as he ran, and leaped the brook, and laid an arrow on the string. When he was within killing distance, he sent his arrow through one of the armed men. Then that struggle around Hiarandi suddenly ceased, and the men fled in all directions, not stopping for their companion; but one of them carried a shaft in his shoulder, and a third bore one in his leg. And then Rolf saw how the thrall had loitered to see what was being done, but he ran again when the men fled. Rolf took a fourth arrow, and shot at the slave, and it stood in the spine of him. Freedom came to the man, but not as he had deemed.

Then Rolf ran to his father, who lay at the foot of the tree. He looked, and saw that Hiarandi was dead.

X

How Rolf Named Witnesses for the Death of Hiarandi

IT HAPPENED THAT on that morning Frodi the Smith had travelled to Cragness to see his kinsmen, and he arrived at the hour of misfortune. For he found Asdis weeping and wringing her hands by the door of the hall, while below on Einar's land Rolf stood over the body of Hiarandi. Then Frodi hastened down to Rolf and wept aloud when he came there. When he could speak, he said:

"Come now, I will help thee bear Hiarandi's body to the house, as is proper."

But Rolf had stood without weeping, and now he said: "Let us bear him only to our own land, for a nearer duty remains than burial." And he and Frodi carried Hiarandi across the brook, and there laid him down; and Asdis covered him with a cloak. Then Rolf said to Frodi:

"Well art thou come, who art my only kinsman, and withal the strongest man in Broadfirth dales. And I would that thou hadst with thee more weapons

than thy whittle. Art thou ready, Frodi, to help me
in my feud?"

Frodi said uneasily: "A man of peace am I, and
never yet have drawn man's blood. I am loth to bare
weapon in any cause. And meseems thou hast no
feud against anyone; for Hiarandi was lawfully slain,
since he was beyond the limit which Snorri set."

"That is to be seen," quoth Rolf, and he went to
the edge of the brook. "Yonder," said he, "stands the
tree where my father was slain, and no step went he
beyond it. (And that tree, until it decayed entirely,
was known as Hiarandi's tree.) Now see," said Rolf,
"if I can throw an arrow so far."

Then he sent an arrow, and it fell short by three
roods; and the second shaft went but two yards farther, so that fourteen yards more were needed. Then
Rolf tried again, and put all his skill and strength
into the effort, yet the arrow fell scarce a foot beyond the second. Rolf dropped the bow and put his
face in his hands.

"I cannot do it," groaned he.

"It is impossible to any man," said Frodi.

"He gives up easily," answered Rolf, "who hath no
heart in the cause. Yet it remains to be seen if there
are not men who can shoot farther than I. Try thou
for me."

Frodi replied: "I am strong for the working of
iron and the lifting of weights, but to shoot with the
bow is another matter. That requires skill rather than
strength."

"But try!" beseeched Rolf.

So Frodi tried, but he failed lamentably. "Said I not," asked he, "that I was not able? And now I say this, that by all thou art accounted the best archer in the district. For last winter, when we tried archery on the ice, and all did their uttermost, only Surt of Ere and Thord of Laxriver shot farther than thou, and that by not so much as a rood. Yet thou art much stronger each month, while they are grown men, and their strength waxes not at all. And if they surpass thee by no more than a rood, no help is in them for this matter."

Rolf knew Frodi spoke wisely, for that man must be found who could shoot three roods farther than himself. But he said: "Would I were the weakest in all Broadfirth dales, if only men might be found to surpass me by so much. But I will not leave this matter, and all the rest shall be done as is right."

So Rolf called Frodi to witness that the man whom he had slain, well known to them both, was a man of Einar's household. And Rolf cast earth upon his face, as a sign that he acknowledged the slaying of him. Then the two bore the body of Hiarandi to the hall, where Asdis prepared for the burial. But Frodi and Rolf went forth and summoned neighbors, men of property, who were not kinsmen of Einar's, to be at Cragness at the following morning. Twelve men were summoned. And the Cragness-dwellers did no more on that day.

But at Fellstead, although there were some wounds to be dressed, men were cheerful. For Hiarandi was gone, and now only a boy stood between Einar and the owning of Cragness; and a boy would be easy to dispose of. The wounded men were sent out of the way, that they might not be accused of the slaying; and when dark came Ondott sent and let bring the body of the man that was slain, and it was buried secretly. Then he and Einar spoke of the future, feeling no guilt on their souls, since all had been done lawfully. And no one noted how the old woman Thurid sat in a corner and crooned a song to herself.

Now these were the words of her song:

> "A tree grows
> And threatens woes.
> Let axes chop so that it fall.
> Let fire burn its branches all.
> Let oxen drag its roots from ground.
> Let earth afresh be scattered round.
> Let no trace stay of oaken tree,—
> So shall good fortune come to thee.
> But if the tree shall stand and grow,
> Then comes to Einar grief and woe."

Yet as she sat muttering the song to herself, Einar went by and bade her be silent, for he was going to sleep. Then she sang to herself:

> "To-night to sleep,
> Some day to weep."

After that she said no more.

But on the morrow those witnesses whom Rolf had summoned came together. They stood at Hiarandi's side, as the custom was, and Rolf named the head wound and the body wound by which he had been slain. Then they went to the place of the slaying; they viewed the tree, and Rolf named it as the spot to which Hiarandi went farthest; and he called on those men to witness that the tree stood there; and the distance was measured, and the tree was put under the protection of the men of the Quarter, so that it might not be cut. Thus all was done that could be done, and the news was taken to Fellstead.

Then Einar said to Ondott: "Where were thy wits? Had we last night destroyed the tree and smoothed the ground, no trial of bow-shooting might ever be made. Now we may be proved in the wrong, and this slaying turn against us."

Ondott had nothing to say, save that no man could shoot that distance. And they dared not now cut the tree.

That night Hiarandi was laid in his cairn, which they made of stones, by the edge of the cliff where all mariners could see it. And he was remembered as the first man in Iceland who lighted beacons against shipwreck, so that those who sailed by prayed for his soul.

XI

Of Rolf's Search for One to Surpass Him with the Bow

TWO VOWS ROLF made before he slept that night: the first was that he would yet show his father's slaying unlawful; the second was that, so long as he might, he would neither stand, sit, nor lie, without weapon within reach of his hand. For Hiarandi might have saved himself had he but had his sword. Asdis and Frodi, who stood by and heard the vows, might not blame him; for such was the custom of those days. Then Rolf begged Frodi to stay with him to help finish the sowing, and that was done. And when the spring work was finished on the farm, then it was within six weeks of the sitting of the Althing. But Rolf felt that the work had to be done, for his mother's sake.

Then Rolf set forth on that quest of his, to find a man to beat him at the bow. First he went to Surt of Ere, and begged him to try skill with him. Then it was seen that Rolf's strength had so waxed during the winter, that Surt overshot him by no more than two

yards. Next Rolf went to Thord of Laxriver, but that
failed completely, for by now Rolf could shoot even as
far as Thord. After that he went about in the dales,
to find men who were good at archery; but though he
heard of many with great names, those men proved to
be nothing helpful to Rolf, for none could surpass
him at all. So he began to learn how much is a little
distance, even so much as a palm's breadth, at the end
of a race or of the fling of a weapon. And time drew
on toward the sitting of the Althing, so that Rolf
feared that he should be able to make out no case
against Einar. At last, after wide wanderings, he got
himself back to Cragness, and sat wearily at home for
three days, with little to say or do.

That third morning Asdis said to him: "Leave,
my son, thy brooding, and let this matter rest for a
while. Over-great are our enemies, yet mayhap in
time our deliverance will come."

Rolf answered nothing but: "Little comes to those
who seek not."

Now Frodi had gone for one night to his smithy,
which was ten miles from Cragness, beyond Hel-
gafell, at the head of Hvammfirth, where there was
a ferry by a little river. When he came back quoth
he: "Yesterday crossed at the ferry those two men
who are most famous in all the South Firths, and
they had a great company with them."

"Who were they?" asked Rolf at once, "and what
kind was their following, whether fighting-men or
not?"

"Fighting-men were they," answered Frodi, "but on a journey of peace. For Kari and Flosi were on their way to visit Snorri the Priest at his hall at Tongue. Great would have been thy pleasure at seeing the brave array."

"Now, would I had been there!" cried Rolf, springing up. "But I would have looked at more than the brave array. So farewell, mother, and farewell, Frodi, for I too go on a visit to Snorri the Priest."

They could not stay him; he took food and a cloak, with his bow, and went out along the firth on that long journey to Tongue. For he said to himself that in that company or nowhere else in Iceland would he find an archer to shoot for him.

Too long is it to tell of that journey, but it was shortened inasmuch as fishermen set Rolf across Hvammfirth. Then he went from Hvamm up to Tongue, and came to the hall of Snorri the Priest. A great sight was that hall, for no other that Rolf had seen was equal to it, and the hall at Cragness might have been set inside it. Long it was, and broad; wide were the porch-doors, and beautiful the pillars that flanked them. Men went in and out, carrying necessaries from the storehouse which stood at another side of the great yard. And so noble was the housekeeping of Snorri the Priest, that at first Rolf feared to enter the hall. But at last he asked a servant:

"Will it be taken well if I enter?"

"Who art thou," asked the man, "not to know that all are welcome at Snorri's house?"

So Rolf went in where all were feasting, for it was the hour of the noonday meal. Many men were there, and none took notice of Rolf, save that when he sat down on the lowest bench one came and offered food. Rolf would take none. He cast his eyes about the place, where twelve fires burned along the middle of the hall, where were seats for many people, and where continually servants went to and fro. All seats were filled save one or two. But at the further end of the hall, on the dais, sat a small man, gray-haired and thin-bearded, with bright eyes of a light blue. And that was Snorri the Priest, the greatest man in all the west of Iceland.

At his sides sat two other men: the one to his right was iron-gray, bearded and strong, a man of sixty summers; and to the left sat a younger man, with no gray in his light hair, slighter in body, and yet of vigorous frame. And it was strange that those two men sat together in peace, who once had been the bitterest of foes. For the older was Burning-Flosi, who had burned Njal in his house; but the other was Kari, Solmund's son, who had been Njal's son-in-law, and alone of all the fighting-men had escaped from that burning. And his vengeance upon the Burners was famous, for he followed them in Iceland, and slew many; and great was his part in the fight at the Althing, as may be read in Njal's saga.

But when the Burners were outlawed and fared abroad, then Kari followed them by land and sea, and slew them where he met them. No other vengeance is like to that which Kari, alone, took for his own son, and for Njal and his sons, Grim the strong, and Helgi the gentle, and Skarphedinn the terrible. But Kari missed Flosi in his searchings; so that Flosi came to Rome, and was absolved from the sin of the Burning, and so journeyed home. But Kari came also to Rome and was absolved from the sin of his vengeance, and went home. Then Kari was wrecked at Flosi's door, and went to his house for shelter, to put his manhood to the proof. But Flosi welcomed him, and they were accorded; and friends they were thenceforth.

Now all this tale was known to Rolf, as it was to all men in Iceland, and as it should be known to all who read of the deeds of great men. So he sat and marvelled at those two, how noble they looked, men who had never done a guileful deed; and in that they were different from Snorri, who had won his place by craft alone. Rolf looked also at those others who sat by the dais, all men of station who looked like warriors, some one of whom might be the man who should help him against Einar. And he took great courage, for there were the men of most prowess in all Iceland.

Now one of the Southfirthers had been telling a story of Grettir the Outlaw, how he flogged Gisli the son of Thorstein with birch twigs. But when the story was ended, Snorri said:

"Mayhap my son Thorod will tell us what he knoweth of Grettir."

Then began a snickering among the servingmen,

and those of Tongue looked mighty wise. But Thorod, Snorri's son, got up from his seat and left the hall, saying he would not stay to be laughed at. When he was gone a great laughter rose, so that Flosi asked to be told the cause of it. Snorri said:

"This will show all how Grettir has wits in his head. Some time ago I was wroth with my son, for he seemed to me not manly enough. So I sent him from me, bidding him do some brave deed ere he returned. And he went seeking an outlaw, to slay him. He found one who had been outlawed for an assault, but he was a lad; and the woman of the house where he worked sent my son further, to find Grettir where he lurked on the hillside. And Thorod found him and bade him fight.

" 'Knowest thou not,' asked Grettir, 'that I am a treasure-hill wherein most men have groped with little luck?'

"But for all that my son would fight. So he smote with his sword, but Grettir warded with his shield and would not strike in return. So at last when he was weary of such doings, Grettir caught up Thorod and sat him down beside him, and said: 'Go thy ways now, foolish fellow, before I lose my patience with thee. For I fear thee not at all, but the old gray carle, thy father, I fear truly, who with his counsels hath brought most men to their knees.' So my son went away, and came home, and because the story pleased me I received him again."

So they laughed again, Southfirthers and West-firthers together, and joyous was the feast. But when all was quiet again, men saw that Snorri wished to speak, and they listened. Snorri called his steward, and said:

"Fetch a stool, and set it here on the dais, for a new visitor hath come to see me."

Then the steward fetched a carved stool, and set it on the dais. He put a cushion in it, and threw a broidered cloth over it. And all grew curious to see who should sit on that stool.

Then Snorri said again: "Few are my kindred on my mother's side, and not in many years hath one entered this hall. But one sits here whose face recalls the features of my mother Thordisa. Let that stranger under my roof who claims to bear the blood of the Soursops, come forward to me!"

Rolf arose, and while all men stared at him, he walked to the dais and stood before Snorri.

XII

Of the Trial of Skill at Tongue

SNORRI ASKED of Rolf: "Art thou the son of Hiarandi my kinsman?"

"His son am I," answered Rolf.

"So must thy father be dead," said Snorri. "For I feared he would break his bounds."

"It is yet to be proven," replied Rolf, "whether he be lawfully slain or no."

Then Flosi said: "Let us hear this tale, for it hath not yet come to our ears. Sit here before us, and tell what hath happened."

So Rolf sat there on the stool which had been prepared, and he told his story. All who sat there listened, and the men of the South Firths drew up close. It was a new thing for Rolf thus to speak before great men, and before fighting-men; but he bore himself well and spoke manfully, forbearing to complain, so that they murmured praise of him. And it seemed to them wrong that he had been so treated, and the younger men grew wroth. When Rolf had finished telling of the death of Hiarandi, one of the Southfirthers sprang up and stood before the dais.

74

That was Kolbein the son of Flosi, and he asked: "May I speak what is in my mind?"

They bade him speak.

"This place on Broadfirth," said Kolbein, "is not so far out of our way when we journey back. Let us make a stop there, and pull this man Einar out of his house, and so deal with him that he shall do no evil hereafter."

This he said with fire, for he was a young man.

But Flosi answered: "Now is seen in thee the great fault of this land, for we are all too ready to proceed unlawfully. And men can know by me how violence is hard repaid." All knew he spoke of the Burning, and of that vengeance which took from him many kinsmen. "Let us do nothing unlawful. What sayest thou, Kari?"

Then Kari said that nothing should be done without the law. And the young man sat down again. But Kari called on Snorri for his opinion.

"Methinks," said Snorri, "that the lad hath some way of his own which may serve."

"If that is all," answered Kari, "then we will help him."

"It is only," said Rolf, "that one of you here will shoot with the bow three roods farther than I. Thus can my father's death be proved unlawful and Einar stand punishable."

With great eagerness the young men sprang up and got their bows. All said they would do their best to help the lad, but it was plain that they regarded the matter an easy one. So Rolf took heart at their confidence. Then all went out to the mead, where was good space for shooting.

"But first," said Kari, "let us get our hand in with shooting at a mark. Then when we are limber we will shoot to show our distance."

So that was done, and all thought that great sport, and a fine opportunity for each to show what man he was. The Southfirthers and the Westfirthers set apples on sticks and shot them off, and they shot next at the sticks themselves, and last they shot at a moving mark. Then they called Rolf to show his skill.

Flosi asked of Kari: "Thinkest thou the lad can shoot?"

"Slender is he," answered Kari, "but strong in the arms and back, and his eye is the eye of an eagle. Our young men will not find their task easy."

Rolf struck the apples, and then the sticks, and then the moving mark. Then they swung a hoop on the end of a pole, and Rolf sent his arrow through it, but most of the others failed.

Kari laughed. "Ye forget," quoth he, "that the lad shoots at birds and cannot afford to lose his arrows. Who among us hath had such training? But now let us try at the distance."

So the ground was cleared for that, and the weaker bowmen shot first, and some good shots were made. Rolf was called upon to say what he thought. He shook his head.

"Ye must do better," he said.

Then better bowmen shot, all those who were there except Kari and Kolbein. Snorri would not shoot, but Flosi did, and a great honor it was deemed that he should oblige the lad. But when all had finished, then Rolf took his bow, and his arrow fell upon the farthest which had been sent, and split it.

Snorri laughed. "So hath my kinsman come here," he said, "and all for naught."

But Kari said: "Kolbein and I have yet to shoot, and we are about alike in skill." So they shot one after the other, and they shot equally, so far that all were pleased, and some ran to measure the distance, finding it three roods and more beyond Rolf's arrow. Many cried that the matter was now settled.

But Snorri said: "Let Rolf shoot once more. Mayhap he hath not yet done his best."

Then Rolf took his bow again, and the arrow flew; it fell less than a rood behind the arrows of Kari and Kolbein.

So it was proved that none there might help Rolf in his need. Then he was greatly cast down; and he wished to go away at once, but they detained him over night. No men could be kinder to him. And in the morning, when he was to start home, they offered him money, but he would take none. So Snorri gave him a cape, and Flosi a belt, and Kari gave a short sword, handsome and well made; much was he honored by those gifts. Snorri lent him a horse to take him to Hvamm, and there boatmen set him again across the firth.

Weary and disheartened, he came to Cragness on the morning of the second day, and without joy he entered the hall. There Asdis met him in great trouble.

"Here has been," said she, "a great man and a rough, who made me feed him. Misfortunes come to us from all sides, for Frodi is away, and the man took our milk-ewe, and has driven it away before him, going towards the fells."

"When was he here?" asked Rolf.

"Not two hours ago."

"I will seek him," said the lad, and turned from the house.

"Nay," cried Asdis in alarm, "I beg thee, go not! For he was huge and fierce of aspect. Thou art too tender to meet such as he. Put up with this matter and let it pass."

"Mother," answered Rolf, "I am sixteen years old, and since the death of my father I am a man in the eye of the law. Wouldst thou have me less than a man in fact?" And he went his way after the robber.

XIII

Of that Robber

ROLF FOLLOWED that man who had stolen the ewe, and the way led first down into the dales, and then upward to the fells. There had been rain and the paths were soft, so that the tracks of man and sheep were clear. It was strange to Rolf that the robber showed such boldness as to go on beaten ways. But when at last he reached the region where all the paths were grassy and tracks could no longer be seen, then Rolf knew not what to do until he met a wayfarer.

"Hast thou seen," asked Rolf, "one who goes driving a ewe?"

"He is not far before thee," answered the man. "But what seekest thou with him?"

"The ewe is mine," said Rolf. "I will have it again."

"Thou art foolhardy," cried the man. "A life is more than a sheep. Turn back!"

"Not I," quoth Rolf, and he went on. Then in a little while he saw the man before him, going without haste behind the ewe. And Rolf marvelled at his confidence, for the man did not even look back to see if he were followed. So Rolf strung his bow and went faster, going quietly until he was but fifty feet behind the man. And then he called to the robber.

That man turned at once, drawing his sword. Grim and harsh was he in face when he found he was followed, but when he saw a lad, alone, then he smiled.

"Seekest thou me?" he asked. And his voice was harsh, like his face, so that he was a man to terrify many.

"That sheep is mine," said Rolf. "Leave it and go thy way."

"Go home, boy!" said the man. "I would not hurt thee."

"Once more," cried Rolf, "I bid thee leave the ewe, else will I strive with thee for it."

"What," sneered the man, "wilt thou set thyself against me? Draw thy sword, then!"

But the robber's sword was long and heavy, while Rolf's was short and light. "Nay," he responded, "but I will hurt thee with my arrows. Take thy shield and defend thyself."

"No shield do I need," sneered the man again, "against such as thou. Shoot, and see if thou canst touch me!"

So great was his contempt that he stung Rolf to the quick. "Let us see, then!" the lad cried. And in great heat of anger, at short range, Rolf drove a shaft at the middle of the man's body. But behold! the man swung his heavy sword as lightly as a wand, and brushed the arrow aside!

"Once more!" quoth he.

And then Rolf shot again, and yet again, but each time the arrow was swept aside. And the robber called with jeers to shoot faster. So Rolf sent his shafts as swiftly as he could, and it was astonishing to see how fast they followed each other; but though he shot half a score of times, each arrow, just as it reached its mark, was brushed aside. Of them all, one touched the clothing on the robber's breast, so that it tore the cloth; and one, sent at the face, scratched the skin ere it was turned. When that was done, the man jeered no more, for he saw that Rolf was closing in.

And what might have happened is not known. But to Rolf, even in his anger to be so foiled, there came admiration of the stranger's skill. "Now," he thought, "such a thing is a marvel, for it is related of the men of old time, but not of the men of to-day. I had not deemed anyone so quick or so strong." Then his own words told him who the man must be; he stopped advancing, and lowered his bow.

But in a twinkle the man dropped his sword and strung his own bow, and he laid an arrow on the string. "Now," cried he, "we have changed about, and can play the game the other way. Perhaps thou also canst guard thyself." He drew the bow. "Art thou minded to try?"

Rolf made no movement to ward himself. "Thou art Grettir the Strong," he said.

"Grettir Asmund's son am I," answered the man, "whom men call Grettir the Strong. Perhaps thou art now the more minded to slay me, even as fools whom I meet from time to time. For nine hundreds in silver is the price set upon my head."

"Nay," answered Rolf, "I would not slay thee."

The man laughed mightily. "I owe my life to thee!" he cried. Then he changed his manner suddenly. "Go, leave me, boy, for my temper is short, and I might do thee a mischief!"

And then he went on his way, still driving the ewe before him; but Rolf remained in that place. After a time the lad gathered those of his arrows which were not broken, and turned back toward his home. But when he looked behind, and saw that a roll of land hid him from Grettir, then he turned again, and followed after the outlaw.

A long time Rolf followed, warily at first, for Grettir looked back once or twice; then the lad might go more boldly. And the outlaw led him up into the hills, where were rocks and crags and much barrenness, a region where men might lurk long and not be found. And Grettir made a halt at a strong place, a shelf on the crags, protected from above by a sheer cliff, and reached only from one side. It seemed as if he had often been there before. While he made a fire, Rolf lay at a distance, and wondered how he might steal nigher. Only one vantage did he see which commanded the outlaw's lair: a great spur of rock which stood out from the cliff, but which it would be hard to reach.

Then Grettir laid himself to sleep while it was yet day, and Rolf crept forward till he was under the spur. From above no man might reach it; yet there were crevices here and there in the rock by which Rolf could climb. So he slung his bow on his back and tried the ascent. But so slow must he climb, for fear of noise, that it was dark when he reached the flat top; and though Grettir was scarce forty feet away, Rolf could not see him at all. So he watched there through the night.

Ever at that little distance he heard Grettir labor in his sleep, and oft the outlaw moaned and groaned. At times he started up and looked abroad, but he could see nothing by the light of the stars. But when dawn came, then Grettir slept peacefully; and when it was broad day he still lay sleeping. His face in sleep was sad and noble, with signs of a hasty temper; his frame was great indeed. He lay so long that Rolf at last strung his bow and shot an arrow into the ground by him. Grettir started from his sleep, grasping his weapons and looking about for his foes. Never in his life Rolf forgot that sight, which few men had seen without ruing it, of Grettir angry and ready for the fray.

But Grettir saw no one, for he looked about on the hillside below him. Then Rolf spoke: "Here am I, Grettir."

Then the outlaw saw him, and put up his shield against a second arrow. Rolf said: "Had I wished, I could have slain thee in thy sleep."

"Rather will I believe," answered Grettir, "that thou has shot thy last arrow, and missed."

Rolf showed him his full quiver, and Grettir lowered his shield. "How camest thou here?" he asked. "I made sure that thou wert gone."

"Not very sure," answered Rolf.

"And how," asked Grettir, "didst thou reach that place? I had weened no man could mount that rock."

"I am but a boy," answered Rolf, "yet men call me Cragsman."

"Now I am well shamed," cried Grettir, "that a boy hath so outwitted me! And this I believe, that thou mightest have slain me; for a good archer I found thee yesterday. Still more will I say, that yesterday I had near suffered a hurt at thy hands, so that I was considering whether to retreat before thee, or to take my shield, and neither have I yet done before a single archer. Now let me ask thee, why didst thou stop shooting then; and why didst thou not slay me here as I lay?"

"Because," answered Rolf, "thou, or no man in Iceland, canst give me the help I need."

"Come down," said Grettir, "and we will eat together."

So they breakfasted together, of dried meat and the milk of the ewe. "How was thy sleep there on the crag?" asked Grettir.

"No worse," answered Rolf, "than thine here on the ledge. Why didst thou sleep so ill?"

Then Grettir answered soberly: "One of my few good deeds is so repaid that I see shapes in the dark, and my sleep is broken. For I slew Glam the ghost who wasted Thorhallstead, but ere I cut off his head he laid on me that spell. So I am a fearsome man in the dark, though in the day no man may daunt me. But what can I do for thee?"

"Let me see," answered Rolf, "if with the bow thou canst shoot farther than I."

"Thou art a vain lad," said Grettir, somewhat displeased. "For that alone comest thou hither?"

"Be not wroth," begged Rolf, "for I have the best of reasons." And he told the story of his father's death and of the need for a good archer. Grettir smiled.

"And couldst thou find no man," asked he, "who is within the law, to do this for thee?"

Then Rolf told of the trial with those Southfirthers at Tongue, and Grettir looked upon him with surprise. "So skilled art thou then?" he asked. "Now string thy bow, and show me how far thou canst shoot."

So Rolf strung his bow, and shot along the hillside, and the arrow fell far away. "Now do I wonder," said Grettir. "Let me see thy bow." And when he had looked on it he said: "That any one could shoot so far with such light gear I had not thought possible. Thou art a good bowman. But what thinkest thou of my bow?"

Rolf took the bow of Grettir in his hand, and a strange weapon it was. For it was shorter than his own bow, and scarcely shaped at all, but was heavy and thick, so that it had seemed not to be a bow, save for the string and notched ends.

"Such a bow," said Rolf, "saw I never."

"Canst thou string it?" asked Grettir.

Then Rolf tried, but he could scarce bend it a little way. Yet Grettir took it and strung it with ease. Then he showed Rolf his arrows, which were heavy, short, and thick, like the bow. He laid one on the string, and drew it to the head, and behold! it rushed forth with a great whir, and with such force that it might pierce a man behind his shield. And it flew far beyond the arrow of Rolf, full five rood further.

"What thou dost with skill," said Grettir, "I do with strength." But Rolf cried with great joy:

"Thou art the man I have been seeking!" Then he asked: "Wilt thou go with me and shoot an arrow before witnesses, to prove that my father was unlawfully slain?"

"That I will," quoth Grettir, "and joyfully too, for I see little of men. Only one thing I require, that safe conduct be promised me to go and come, for I have enemies in thy dales."

"How shall I get thee safe conduct?" asked Rolf.

"It must be granted," answered Grettir, "by the Quarter Court at the Althing."

Then they talked the matter over, and Grettir advised Rolf once more to seek Snorri the Priest, to find what steps should be taken. Then it was bespoken where Rolf should meet Grettir again, and the outlaw offered to lay out in the hills north of the Thingvalla, in the valley of the geysirs, and await tidings of the outcome of the suit.

"Now," said Rolf, when he was ready to go, "keep the ewe for thy kindness's sake."

"Do thou take her," answered Grettir. "For had I known that thy mother was a widow, I would never have taken the sheep. And the first booty is this, which ever I rendered again."

So Rolf returned toward home driving the ewe; and when he reached the highway which led to the South Firths, there came riding a company, Kari and Flosi and their followers, and Snorri the Priest was with them. They asked tidings. Then he told them of Grettir, and those three chiefs left their horses, and sat down with Rolf on the fell a little way from their company; they had talk what was to be done. For Snorri declared he saw a flaw in the case, since Grettir was an outlaw, and no outlaw had ever yet come into a suit at law. But at last he said:

"Now go thy way, and summon Einar with a formal summons. [And he taught Rolf the form.] But be thou sure that no mention is made of Grettir. And I believe that, since no such case has ever yet been tried, it can lawfully be brought about that Grettir may shoot."

Then those chiefs went their way, and Rolf went his, and he came back to Cragness.

XIV

How Rolf and Einar
Summoned Each Other

BECAUSE OF THE state of matters at Cragness,
Frodi the Smith journeyed there frequently to see
his relatives. Here it must be told what kind of man
he was. He was tall and heavy-jointed, with a long
neck and a long face, and somewhat comic to look
upon. Frodi the Slow was he by-named, for his move-
ments were cumbersome and his mind worked slowly.
But since that affair at the sheep-fold, many called
him Whittle-Frodi.

Now Rolf sends for him one day, and tells him all
that had happened, and how he was sure of making
Einar an outlaw. And he asks Frodi to go with him
to the house of Einar, to be witness to the summons.

Then said Frodi: "Let me say what I think of this
affair. First thou shouldst ask a peaceful atonement.
For in the beginning it seems that there is danger to
thee, so great is the strength against thee. And in
the second place such continual blood-feuds as daily
go on are unchristian, and evil for the land."

88

Then Rolf was thoughtful. "Shall I have done all my seeking for nothing?" he asked. "More than that, shall I take money for my father's slaying?"

"It is the custom of the land," said Frodi, "and many men do it for the sake of peace."

"I heard Flosi say at Tongue," said Rolf, "how strife between neighbors was the greatest bane of this land. And I am half minded to do as thou sayest. But why has not Einar offered me atonement, if any is to be paid? I tell thee, hard is his heart, and he is glad!"

"At least," begged Frodi, "let me ask Einar what he will do."

"So I will," answered Rolf, "and a great sacrifice I make, to lay aside my grief and vengeance. Nay, I even break my vow which I made before thee. But I think only scorn will be thy portion, and matters will be made worse."

Then they went together to the house of Einar, and were seen from the hall as they entered the yard, and men came and stood in the porch as they approached. There were Einar and Ondott, and other men of the household. All bore weapons. But no one spoke when the cousins stood before them. "Will no one here give us welcome?" asked Frodi.

Ondott mimicked Frodi's slow voice, and said: "Be welcome." The men of Einar laughed.

"Laugh not," said Frodi mildly. "Now, Einar, it is known how Hiarandi came by his death, and men say thou art responsible therefor."

"I was not by at his slaying," answered Einar.

Said Rolf: "What is done by a man's servants, with his knowledge, is as his deed."

And Frodi said: "Were it not better to atone Rolf for the death of his father, rather than have bad blood between neighbors? For thou knowest this, that some day a man may be found to shoot an arrow beyond that little oak."

Now Einar was plainly smitten by the answer of Frodi, and the scorn went from his face, and he thought. And here may be seen how the evil which a bad man does is not half so much in quantity as the good which he mars. For Ondott Crafty saw what was in Einar's mind, and he spoke quickly.

"An award may be given, Einar," said he, "which will honor you both. Shall I utter it?"

Now Einar was accustomed to the bitter jokes of Ondott, and when he thought he saw one coming, he forgot his design of peace, and said: "Utter the award."

"But does Rolf agree to it?" asked Ondott.

"I will hear it," answered Rolf. "But if thou meanest to scoff, think twice, lest in the end it be bad for thee."

Meanwhile some of the women of the household had come out of the hall at its other end, by the women's door, and now stood near to hear what was said. Helga the daughter of Einar was there, but she hung back; nearest of all stood Thurid the crone, listening closely.

"Now this I would award," said Ondott, "If I were in thy place, Einar. Thy son Grani is abroad, in the fostering of the Orkney earl; but some day he will come home, and then will need men to serve him. Let Rolf give up his holding and become thy man; so canst thou protect him from all harm. Then when thy son returns Rolf shall be his bow-bearer, and shall be atoned by the honor for the death of his father."

Some laughed, but not for long, and so far was this from a jest that the most were silent. Then Thurid chanted:

> "For Einar's son shall Rolf bear bow,
> Which in the end shall bear most woe?"

But none paid attention, for Rolf was gathering himself to speak. And he cried; "Ill jesting is thine, Ondott! Now hear what I am come hither to say: Outlaw shall Einar be made, for that man is found who can make the shot beyond the little oak. And thus I summon Einar."

So he recited the summons. He named the deed and the place, and the wounds of which Hiarandi had died. He named witnesses, those householders who had already been summoned. And he called Einar to answer for the deed before the Westfirther's Court at the Althing.

Ondott alone laughed when the summons was spoken in full. "So here are come a boy and a peaceling," quoth he, "to pick a quarrel with men."

"Heed him not," said Frodi to Rolf, "for he seeks cause to draw sword on thee."

Then Rolf made no answer to Ondott but he and Frodi turned away and started to go home. Ondott whispered to Einar: "A spear between the shoulders will settle this matter for good." And he signed to Hallvard that he should have his spear ready to throw. Einar stood irresolute.

But the maid Helga went forward quickly and walked by Rolf's side. "May I go with thee to the gate?" she asked.

Great anger possessed him against all of Einar's house, but the sight of her astonished him, and he said she might come. In silence they went to the gate of the yard; then Helga stood there in the way while those two from Cragness went homeward. And Einar had already bidden that no violence be done, for fear of harming his daughter. He went into the hall and sat down in his seat, brooding over the outcome.

Ondott said: "Too squeamish art thou."

Einar said: "If thou findest me not a way out of this, it will go ill with thee."

Now a way out of that would have been hard to find, had not one day Ondott met that man who had set Rolf on the right road as he pursued Grettir. Said the man: "So thy neighbor Rolf won his sheep again from Grettir the Strong. That was a great deed!"

Then Ondott learned of the stealing of the sheep, and how Rolf had been seen driving it home again.

He thought, and knew who must be that man who would shoot for Rolf. Then he went homeward with a light heart.

"Now," said he to Einar, "thy defense is sure. But come with me, and we will summon Rolf for those wounds he dealt, and that man he slew, when Hiarandi was slain."

"No court," answered Einar, "will punish Rolf for that." And he would not go, though he gave Ondott permission to go in his stead. Ondott took a witness and went to Cragness, where Rolf and Frodi were at work in the yard. Ondott recited the summons; Rolf and Frodi went on with the work, and answered naught.

And now all is quiet until men ride to the Althing.

XV

Of Suits at the Althing

ROLF JOURNEYED to the Althing, and as he went he fell in with the company of Snorri the Priest, and travelled with them. Snorri heard how the summons had gone, and he asked whether Rolf had said anything of Grettir. Rolf answered that he had not. Then he told of the summons which On-dott had made, and Snorri laughed. It was not many days before they came to the Thingvalla, and Rolf saw that great wonder of Iceland.

For from the plain on which they journeyed a large part had fallen clean away, many yards down, and it lay below like the bottom of a pan. The Great Rift was the name of the western precipice, and there was no way down save by one steep path; Snorri had held that path on the day of the battle at the Althing, nor would he let Flosi and the Burners escape that way. When Rolf had got down to the plain, he saw all the booths for the lodging of those who came to the Althing, ranged along the river. He saw the places where the Quarter Courts were held, and he went to the Hill of Laws, where the Fifth Court sat to hear appeals. Now the Hill of Laws is cut off from the plain by deep rifts, and men showed Rolf where, to save his life, Flosi had leaped one rift at its narrowest part, and that was a great deed. Other wonders were to be seen. Then on the second day the sitting of the courts began, and Rolf watched closely for the calling of his suit. But that came not until the sitting was near its end.

Now Snorri conducted the case of Rolf, and all went in due order. Einar answered what was said against him, that he was not present at the slaying of Hiarandi. Snorri called on the court to say whether Einar were not answerable, because his men did the deed. The judges said he was. Then it came to proving whether or not the slaying were illegal, and Snorri said that a man had been found who could shoot the distance. And this he asked of the judges:

"Is it not true that when, before witnesses, an arrow is shot from the boundary and falls beyond the tree, that will prove the slaying unlawful?"

"That is so," said the judges.

"Now say further," demanded Snorri. "Is it not true that in the moment when the slaying is proved unlawful, the guilt of Einar is established, so that no suit at law is needed?"

"That also is true," answered the judges.

"Now," said Snorri, "one last thing do I ask, whether or not he who goes to make the proof by shooting an arrow, may go and come freely, whatsoever man he be?"

"We see no reason why this may not be so," said the judges.

"Now give that decision here aloud in the open court," required Snorri.

But Einar arose and said: "One exception only shall I ask to this, that no outlaw be allowed to take part in this suit, by shooting the arrow."

Then said Snorri to Rolf, "They have learned of Grettir." He said to the judges: "Well do I know that no outlaw is ever allowed to give witness in court, nor to sit on juries. But no such case as this has ever arisen, and it seems to me that an outlaw might be permitted to shoot."

Then there was great talking on both sides, for the greater part of an hour: it would be tedious to tell what was said. But the end was, that the judges were divided, so the question was referred to the Lawman. And his answer was, that no outlaw might take part in a law matter in any way whatsoever. There was an end to Rolf's hopes to prove Einar guilty by the means of Grettir.

But Snorri called all men to witness that when some day a man might be found to shoot the distance, then Einar was guilty without going to law. Now men began to whisper and say that the end of Grettir's outlawry was but four years off, and then Rolf could be justified. So Einar tried to have a limit of three years set on that time when it was lawful to try the shooting; but Snorri strove mightily against that, and that question went to the Lawman, and he said that seven years should be the limit.

That was the end of the suit, and Rolf got no satisfaction at all. One more thing was done on that day, for Snorri went to Einar where he stood with Ondott, and he asked of the second suit, for which Rolf had been summoned. Ondott spoke for Einar.

"We shall not bring that suit."

"That is well," said Snorri, "for ye had no case, and I could have a fine laid on you if the case was brought falsely." Then he took Rolf with him to his booth.

But here is the trick which Ondott had prepared. For the next day was the last of the sittings, and Snorri was busy with many matters; but Rolf stayed at the booth, much cast down. Then toward the sunset hour the cases were all finished, and men left the courts, all save the judges, who stayed for the formal closing. Then Ondott brought forward the case against Rolf, and summoned him into court, but no one was there to tell either Snorri or the lad. Nevertheless it was the law that the suit might go on, because lawful summons had been given. And Einar stood up and said:

"I take witness to this, that I give notice of a suit against Rolf Hiarandi's son, in that he slew by a body wound, by an arrow, my herdsman Thorold. I say that in this suit he ought to be made a guilty man, an outlaw, not to be fed, not to be forwarded, not to be helped or harbored in any need. I say that all his goods are forfeited, half to me, and half to the men of the Quarter, who have a right by law to take his forfeited goods; I give notice of this suit in the Quarter Court into which it ought by law to come. I give notice in the hearing of all men on the Hill of Laws. I give notice of this suit to be pleaded now, and of full outlawry against Rolf Hiarandi's son."

All that was said in the manner laid down by law. Then Einar pushed the case, and no one was there to answer him. All steps were taken then and there, and judgment was called for and given, and in his absence Rolf was made full outlaw, and his goods were declared forfeited. Not till the court had risen, and nothing might be done, was the news brought to Snorri and Rolf.

Snorri was angry that he had been tricked, yet he could see no way to help himself. This one thing he brought about, that the judges declared that Rolf, outlaw though he was, might shoot to prove his innocence, if he might but get himself safely to the spot. And Snorri sought to comfort Rolf, but the lad was dazed.

"The farm is lost!" he cried.

"Thou canst win it back," answered Snorri. "Thou art young and thy strength will grow. Before the seven years are past thou canst make that shot."

"Nay," said Rolf. "I can never do it until I find some bow as strong as Grettir's, yet which a common man may string. Never have I found a bow too stiff for me, save his alone."

"Skill may beat strength," quoth Snorri. "Somewhere mayest thou find the bow thou dreamest of."

"Where?" demanded Rolf.

Snorri was silent, for he feared no such bow was to be found.

Rolf sighed. "And my mother?" he asked next.

"She shall live with me at Tongue. And now," said Snorri, "meseems best that thou goest home at once. Thou knowest all that is to be done?"

"I know," replied Rolf; and Snorri believed him, because to the Priest all the ways of the law were so familiar that it seemed all men must know them. Yet Rolf did not know, and they meant different things.

"Shall I lend thee money," asked Snorri, "or hast thou enough?"

"I have plenty," said Rolf; yet he had only enough for the journey, whereas much more was needed. Then Rolf took his leave of Snorri, and gave him his thanks; and taking his horse, he went from the Thingfield by the path up the Great Rift. And he passed two men of Einar's, who spoke together that they were to start very early in the morning. From the top of the Rift Rolf looked down on that plain where all men were still busy, and which in years had brought misfortune on all his family. Then at last he went his way.

Now those men of Einar's went to their booth, and told that they had seen Rolf departing. "Hasten back at once," said Ondott, "and find what direction he takes." And they went and watched.

"He went northwest," said they, "and he took not the straight track toward home."

"Then he is gone elsewhere," quoth Ondott, and seemed glad. "Hurry, all of you, for he delivers himself into our hands."

Meanwhile Rolf went northwest to the valley of the geysirs, and on the second day found Grettir the Strong cooking his food at a boiling spring.

XVI

The Act of Distress

ROLF TOLD GRETTIR all that had happened, and much was the outlaw disappointed thereat. For he had counted upon going again among men, and had hoped to win glory from the shooting, so he was sorry on his own account. But also he consoled the boy. For he spoke of the great world over the sea, how there were places and peoples to be seen, and fame to be won. This is clearly seen by those who read the story of Grettir, that all his life he sought fame, and his fate was lighter to him because he knew men would sing of him after his death. But no such thoughts uplifted Rolf, since he grieved for his mother and for the loss of the farm, and it seemed no pleasure to go abroad.

"Now," said he, "far rather would I stay here in this island, until the time of outlawry is past. Why may I not stay with thee?"

"Knowest thou not," asked Grettir, "that if one fares abroad the outlawry is for three years, but if one stays it is twenty? And that is a third of most men's lifetime."

"Yet," said Rolf, "I am minded to do it." For he cared not what happened to him.

"Now," said Grettir, "listen to me, and learn what it means to be an outlaw. No man will take thee within his house, so soon as he knows who thou art. So must thou live in the open, like a beast, or else make hiding-places for thyself. And a miserable life it becomes after a while. No man mayest thou trust, lest he take thy head. Well do I know that Gisli thy ancestor lived an outlaw, fourteen years; yet he lived in holes and caves, and was slain at the end. He was the greatest outlaw of Iceland before me, save only Gunnar of Lithend, who tried to stay in his home and was slain. But I have maintained myself sixteen years, and miserable have they been. Too tender art thou of years and frame to bear the life. Moreover, I know my mother mourns me at home. Think then of thine, and put this idea from thee!"

Then Rolf was ashamed that he had ever thought of such a thing. So he spent a night with Grettir, there among the geysirs, and wonderful were the things that he saw. And in the morning they cooked again at the boiling spring. Then, as they sat eating, Grettir said by chance:

"Thou saidst thou art poor. Did Snorri give the money for the priest's dues, and the court's?"

"What are those dues?" asked Rolf.

Grettir cried: "Has no money been paid for thine outlawry?"

"None by me," answered Rolf.

"And thy neighbor Einar," asked Grettir. "What was he doing when thou camest away?"

"They were preparing for departure, so that I heard a groom say they would start before sunrise in the morning."

Then Grettir sprang up, and went and caught Rolf's pony; he saddled it, and brought it to the lad. "Go home!" he cried. "Too little dost thou know of the law. For if those dues were paid, then thou hadst a year in which to take ship. But they are not paid, so thy enemy can make thee full outlaw ten days after the rising of the Althing, by executing the act of distress at thy house. Three days are gone already, and thou art far from home. For this was Einar hastening away. Now take my advice, and go south, and ship thence."

"Nay," answered Rolf, "first I must see my mother, and perhaps I can reach home in time. Now fare thee well, Grettir. When thy outlawry is finished, then thou shalt gain me my property again."

But Grettir said nay to that. "Well do I know," said he, "that we two shall never meet again. For from here I go to the island of Drangey, to keep myself if I may until my outlawry is over. No stronger place is there in Iceland for defence. But Hallmund the Air-sprite, my friend, foretold I should never come out of my outlawry. Thus I shall never again mix in this affair of thine."

Rolf could answer nothing.

"And in my turn," said Grettir, "thus I foretell thy

fate. No man shall help thee here. With thine own strength and craft must thou regain thine own, or never more be master of thy father's hall!"

Then Rolf was heavy-hearted as he bade Grettir farewell. And Grettir did as he had said: He went to his home at Biarg, and went thence with his brother Illugi to Drangey. How he fared there may be read in the Grettir's Saga. But Rolf fared west to his home. He had lost much time, as Grettir had feared; yet as he neared Cragness on the eleventh day after the rising of the Althing he saw no one, and it was just noon. And only at high noon might the act be executed which would make him full outlaw. So he rode into the yard.

Then there stepped out to meet him from the house Ondott Crafty, who came forward with a greeting. He spoke well to the boy, and bade him alight, yet seemed to wish to get very near. Rolf dismounted on the further side of his horse. "What doest thou here?" he asked.

"Einar hath sent me," said Ondott, still coming closer. "He biddeth thee come to his house, where somewhat can be said concerning this outlawry of thine, to make it easier for thee."

But then Asdis came running from the house. "Flee!" she cried. "Einar and his men are at the crags, and there they make thee outlaw. Flee!"

Then Ondott snatched at Rolf with his lean arms, but the lad felled him with a buffet. Rolf would have mounted his horse again to get away, but men appeared at the gate of the yard, so that there was no way out. Then Rolf passed quickly into the hall, and kissed his mother farewell, and leaped from a window at the other side, meaning to gain the cliffs. His way was all but clear; for spies had seen Rolf's coming and reported it to Einar, who sent his men to seize the lad. They had gone to right and left around the hall, while Einar alone completed the act of distress at the crags; for thus the law said: it must be done at a barren spot where no shade fell, not far from the house of the outlaw. And Einar completed the act, and started toward the house. He alone stood between Rolf and his escape. So Rolf ran at him, drawing his sword.

But Einar fled when he saw the lad's steel. Then Rolf ran up behind, put his sword between Einar's legs, and tripped him. Einar rolled over on his back.

"Mercy!" cried he, and made no attempt to ward himself.

Rolf laid the flat of his sword against Einar's forehead; he shrank from the cold steel, but still did not struggle.

"Now," quoth Rolf, "I go across the sea, yet thou shalt hear from me again. And if I meet in the outlands thy son, of whom thou boastest, I promise thee to put this sword to his forehead, but with the edge, and to draw his blood."

By that, the men of Einar were close at hand. Rolf ran to the crags and let himself down at a place which he knew well. When men with spears came to the edge and looked after him, nothing of him was seen.

XVII

Rolf and Frodi Fare Abroad

ROLF COMES to Frodi where he works in his smithy, there at the head of Hvammfirth. Now the weather is rough, and a strong sea rages among the islands at the mouth of the firth, and the tide-rips are bad. Rolf comes into the smithy, and Frodi greets him well.

"How went thy suit at the Althing?" asks he.

Then Rolf tells him all, how he was now an outlaw, and how he escaped. "And men are out to catch me, for as I came down over the hill, I met one who said that armed men were at the ferry below, waiting for someone. Now lend me thy boat, Frodi, that I may cross to Hvamm, and seek passage on that ship which is there outfitting."

"Remain with me overnight," answered Frodi, "for the wind is rough." But Rolf would not stay. "Then," said Frodi, "I will row with thee, to help against the wind, and coming back I can row easily alone."

"Thou wouldst thus come into danger for forwarding an outlaw," replied Rolf, and on no account would he suffer Frodi to go. So perforce Frodi lent him the boat, and they bade each other Godspeed, and Rolf set out.

That was a hard row in the face of the wind, yet Rolf got safely to Hvamm. Then, desiring that his enemies should think him dead, he set the boat adrift, and oars separately, and saw the waves carry them from the shore. Then he went on his way to the ship which was fitting for the outward voyage; and because it was the law that no shipmaster might refuse passage to an outlaw, Rolf was sure of safety. As he went he met a man of Snorri the Priest, and Rolf sent by him a message to his master. "Forget not thy promise to keep my mother till my return." And so he came to the ship, and was sheltered.

But that boat drifted across the firth, and the wind and tide brought it again to Frodi's smithy, where it lay and beat upon the beach. Frodi went out and drew it up, and knew it as his own, and believed that Rolf was drowned. He went back to his smithy, and sat there weeping.

Then came that way men of Einar's, Hallvard and Hallmund, with Ondott Crafty; and seeing they were three, and Frodi so mild of temper, they went into the smithy to taunt him with the misfortunes of Rolf. Because he wept, they fell to laughter, and asked him: "Why weepest thou, Whittle-Frodi?"

Frodi told them that Rolf was dead. "For he took my boat to row across the firth, and now is the boat come empty to land, without oars or thole-pins."

Then they laughed the more, and taunted him

grievously, saying they were glad at the news, and mocking his weeping. So Hallmund came near, and put his hand on Frodi, calling him a fool. Frodi seized the hand, and rose, and they all saw his face was changed.

"Never in my life," said Frodi, "have I been angry till now!" He drew the man to him, and snapped the bones of his arm; then he raised him and cast him at Hallvard, so that the two fell, but Ondott remained standing. "Now, Ondott," quoth Frodi, "here is the whittle which once thou badst me draw. Let us see if it will cut!" But when he drew the whittle, Ondott fled, and the others scrambled together out of the smithy.

Then Frodi was afraid of the law, for he thought: "They will make me an outlaw for this assault." So he took his boat, and got new oars and thole-pins. Then he fetched his money from his sleeping loft, and fared across Hvammfirth to that same ship where Rolf was. Great was his joy when he saw Rolf.

"What dost thou here?" asked Rolf.

"I will go with thee," answered Frodi. Then he paid the shipmaster his faring, and paid Rolf's also. Two days thereafter they sailed down Broadfirth, and saw Cragness at a little distance. The cairn of Hiarandi was to be seen at the edge of the cliff, but many persons were at work in the field. Rolf knew that his enemies had already set up their household there; but the ship took him, heavy-hearted, east over the sea.

XVIII

How Those Two Came into Thraldom

TWO EARLS RULED in the Orkneys: Brusi and Thorfinn, half-brothers. Of the islands, two thirds were under Brusi, the elder; but besides his third Thorfinn had inherited Caithness and Sunderland in Scotland from his grandfather the Scot king. So Thorfinn lived on those lands, and Brusi guarded all the isles; but Thorfinn complained that the guard was ill-kept, since vikings harried oft in the isles, coming from Norway or Denmark.

There was a man named Ar the Peacock, who was a thane of Brusi the Earl and lived on the Mainland of Orkney. Now the Mainland of Orkney is an island, and Ar ruled its northern end, having charge of the tribute to the Earl and the keeping of order. He lived at that place called Hawksness in Hawkdale, below the downs and sheepwalks, where is good harbor in winter. Forty men he kept, and a war-ship; his hall was great, and there was a stone church close by; fisher-folk and farmers lived in the same settlement.

110

Ar was a vain man and fond of show, kindly but weak. Because he had no child he had taken to him a lad to foster, who was called Grani the Proud, Ar's Fosterling. Grani was tall and fair, of sixteen summers, skilled in games but ignorant of war. He was dear to his foster-father's heart, and Ar could deny him nothing.

That war-ship of Ar's was for the ward of the isles, and Ar kept it at all times in readiness. One day news came that vikings were on the west coast, plundering and burning. Ar sent for Sweyn, the master of his ship.

"Thou shalt take the best of thy men," said Ar, "and search for those vikings. And because Earl Thorfinn has complained that our work is ill-done thou shalt take all pains."

Sweyn said he would.

Then Grani stood before Ar, and said: "Thou hast many times promised I should go a-fighting. Now may I go with Sweyn, or wilt thou put me off yet another time?"

Ar remembered that he had heard of but one viking-ship, so he said: "Thou mayest go."

"Thou hast promised me thralls when the next captives are taken. May I choose them from this ship?"

"Two thralls mayest thou have," answered Ar, "but all Orkneymen are to be freed."

When they made ready to go, Ar said to Sweyn that Grani should be guarded in the fight, and

Sweyn promised to look well to that. They went on board and sailed round into the open sea; there they passed first the great cliffs, and then cruised along the shore, looking for the ship of the vikings.

Now the ship of those chapmen who had given passage to Rolf and Frodi had a good voyage; those two Broadfirthers were the only Icelanders aboard. To them the Orkneyingers boasted much of their land.

"In spite of what ye say," quoth Rolf to them, "the Orkneys are no such safe place as Iceland, as I see clearly, now that we are nearing land."

"In what dost thou see it?" asked the others.

"With us are no sea-robbers," answered Rolf, "but ye have set a watch against vikings, and fear them."

This the Orkneyingers could not deny, for they had kept a look-out ever since they had neared the land. Yet all their care did not avail them, for they met a ship in the Pentland Firth, a war-ship, weather-stained and hardy; shields hung along its sides, and it sailed swiftly. When the chapmen saw the shields taken from the rail, they knew that was a viking-ship. So the chapmen prepared to defend themselves. Rolf got ready to fight; but when the vikings drew near, Frodi sat himself down on a rowing bench, and looked troubled.

"Wilt thou not fight?" asked the shipmaster.

Frodi answered: "It is not clear to me what I should do."

"Shame on thee," cried the other, "if thou wilt not fight for the men who harbored thee!"

So Frodi, all without arms, stood up as the two ships came together, and knew not where to place himself. The vikings came leaping aboard, and all began fighting in confusion; but the vikings were many and were well armed, and the chapmen had no leader. Men fell dead at Frodi's side, and a viking came at him with brandished sword. Frodi caught him and hurled him into the water.

Then he took those other vikings who came near him, and cast them overboard one after another; "and it is no affair of mine," thought he, "if they cannot swim." And he cleared a space about him, but one from a distance cast at him a throwing-axe; it struck him flatwise on the head, and down he fell.

By this time the chapmen were ceasing to fight; but Rolf saw Frodi fall, and fought the harder, to avenge him. The vikings penned him by the rail, yet he broke through them; then when he passed near where Frodi had fallen, Frodi rose up and caught Rolf by the waist, and said: "Now sit we down comfortably here together, for we have done our part." That was the end of the fight, for no men fought more, and the vikings gave peace to them.

Now men began to shout from the water, where they were swimming. Three were hauled up over the side. "How many," asked Rolf of Frodi, "threwest thou over?"

Frodi turned white and would not answer.

Then the vikings despoiled the ship of the chapmen and set her adrift, but the captives were set to row the war-ship. Rolf and Frodi toiled at one oar together, and sore was the labor, but not for long. For on the third day, as they rowed under a bright sky with no wind, they heard a clamor among the vikings, who cried that a long ship was bearing down on them—an Orkney ship, great in size. Some of the vikings snatched their shields from the bulwarks and armed themselves; but many, crying that no mercy would be shown, would take no shields, and instead cast off their shirts of mail, preparing to go into battle baresark.

"Never have I seen that," said Rolf, "though much have I heard of it." For Northmen, in danger of death, often went into battle bare of armor, fighting with fury and mindless of wounds. They believed that thus they came surely into Valhalla; but that was a custom of the heathen, and was not done by Christian folk.

Rolf and Frodi were tied to their bench, and saw nothing of the Orkneymen as they came up astern. But at last the splash of oars was heard; next a grapple came flying aboard; then of a sudden the Orkney ship loomed alongside, and she was a big ship indeed. So tall was she that the vikings could not board her; but from her the Orkneymen sent down arrows, stones, and spears. Bodies of men fell among the rowers' benches, and Rolf and Frodi took each a shield, sat close together, and warded themselves against weapons. Then the Orkneyingers, having cleared the waist of the viking-ship of fighters, came tumbling aboard.

That was a fight with method, for the Orkneymen in two parties drove the vikings to the stem and the stern, and so either slew them or thrust them into the sea. Very hot was the fighting, but it was short; the sixth part of an hour was not over when the fighting was finished.

Now that Orkney ship was the ship of Ar the Peacock, and they who led the fighting were Sweyn and Grani. Sweyn drove the vikings to the bow; but Grani led those who fought in the stern, and two old fighting-men warded him, one on either side. Grani did not know that they were guarding him. When the fighting was finished, Sweyn and Grani met in the waist, near where Rolf sat. Sweyn asked Grani if he had any wound.

Grani said nay thereto. "But I gave wounds, and this has been a great fight."

"Now," said Sweyn, "let us free those who worked at the oars."

"Remember," answered Grani, "that I am to have thralls from the captives."

But of those who had been taken with the ship, it was found that all the vikings were either dead or sore wounded; and all the rowers were Orkneymen save only Rolf and Frodi.

"No Orkneymen can I give thee as thrall," said Sweyn.

Grani answered: "Then I take the two others."

Then Rolf stood up and said: "Icelanders are we. Since when are Icelanders enthralled in the Orkneys, and why is this injustice?"

"Ye are captives," said Grani. Sweyn took him aside to speak with him; but he would not listen, and said, pouting: "Ar promised me."

"Take them then," replied Sweyn.

Grani said to Rolf and Frodi: "Ye are my thralls; I will treat you well. What are your names?"

Rolf answered: "Rolf hight I."

"Of what father and what place?"

"A thrall," answered Rolf, "hath no father and no home."

Frodi replied in like manner.

"It is plain to see," said Sweyn, "that these two should be free men."

"Let them win their freedom, then," answered Grani.

Then a division of men was made, and Sweyn took the chapmen with him in the large ship, but Grani stayed on board the viking-ship as its master. They sailed together for the Orkney coast.

When night came Grani called Rolf and Frodi, and bade them watch by turns while he slept. "I will be a good master so long as ye serve me well."

Rolf thought Grani to be about his age, yet not so old in mind. Much pleased was Grani to own thralls. He seemed kindly, but petulant and uncertain.

XIX

Now Men are Shipwrecked

THOSE TWO SHIPS sailed together, all that day; but in the night they became separated, for there was a little wind. In the morning Grani's ship was close to a shore, and that was the Mainland of Orkney. For miles great cliffs stood up out of the water, the wind fell, and there was a long ground-swell. Then said Grani:

"Often have I seen these cliffs from above; now it will be sport to see them from below. Put in close, and sail along under the cliffs."

Those two old men who had warded him in the fight both spoke to him, saying it were better to keep away. But Grani pouted and gave his order again. "All men say," quoth he, "that the water is deep there, and no harm can befall."

Then they sailed along under the cliffs, and a grand sight that was, to see them high above and stretching far ahead. Rolf stood in the bow, and he looked first up at the cliffs, and then down into the green water. There came a great wave, larger than the others, and after it the water fell away. Just before the ship, Rolf saw a rock break the water with scarcely a ripple, for it was very sharp; seaweed floated around its sides. Another wave came and lifted the ship up, and the rock disappeared as if it had sunk down. Rolf shouted in warning.

But the wave passed, the ship rushed down into the hollow, and struck the rock. The planks tore apart beneath the bow, and all heard the splintering; then the water poured in, a wave lifted the ship, and she slid back into deep water. She began to sink.

There was scarcely time to throw over oars and shields, and to leap after them into the water. The ship went down; the men were swimming, there under the wall of rock. They swam toward the cliff, and those who swam worst clung to the oars. But the cliff rose sharp from the water, only hand-hold was to be had, and the waves bruised the men as they tried to support themselves. Eighteen men in all were there, and they swam in a line along the cliff for an hour, until at last they found a foothold where a shelf of rock jutted under water, and all might stand waist deep.

Then one of the men asked: "Is the tide coming or going?"

They watched to find out, and at last it was sure: the tide was coming. It rose above their waists, so that the smaller men were lifted by the waves; and it was lucky that there was no storm, for they would all have been killed. The tide rose still higher, and men began to look anxious. There they stayed half an hour more, and the sea-otters swam about and looked at them.

Frodi said to Rolf: "What dost thou think, and why look'st thou so at the cliffs above us?"

"They seem to me like the cliffs at home. Were we there I could climb up."

"Seest thou no way here?" asked Frodi.

"I see two ways," answered Rolf, "yet neither seems good."

Grani asked: "What are my thralls saying?"

"The water," said Rolf, "will take thy thralls from thee."

But one of the men had heard what had been said, and told Grani. Grani cried: "Why dost thou not try the climb?"

"Send one of those," answered Rolf, "who cares to save his life." This he said of a set purpose, for of the men some were heavy and some were old. They all shook their heads and said they could not win to the top of the cliff. Grani said:

"I will give thee thy freedom if thou wilt save us."

"Is there a farm above?" asked Rolf.

One of the men said: "Within a mile."

Rolf still stayed where he was. "Why dost thou not go?" cried Grani.

"What of the freedom of my fellow?" asked Rolf.

"He also shall be free," answered Grani.

Then Rolf essayed to climb the cliff by the way which seemed surest; he went up quickly until they lost sight of him, so that they began to say that now he was at the top, and would soon bring a rope. Then something fell with a great splash in the water.

"He hath reached the top and thrown down a rock," cried the men.

But that was Rolf himself, for he had fallen from near the top; presently they saw his head. All breathless and bruised, he swam to them and waited a while; then he sought to climb by the other way, and that was more in sight of the others; marvellous climbing they agreed it was. After a while he went again out of their sight, and in the end they heard him hail. So they were sure he was at the top. Then they waited for him to bring the rope, and the water rose to the breastbone of Frodi, who was tallest; but it was at the chin of the shortest, who had to float, while Frodi held him. They stayed there a long time, and the water rose still higher; it was cold, and some of the men grew very faint. At last shouts were heard, and a rope came dangling down.

Then the shortest man climbed the rope, and he was glad. But others were too weak to climb, and had to be drawn up, one after another. Grani would not go, but sent up the men in the order of their height. When he and Frodi alone were left, Grani said to Frodi: "Go thou next."

"Great is thy pride," answered Frodi, "and thou wishest to do a brave deed, yet thy strength is not sufficient. For see, thou art blue about the lips, and I am holding thee upright. How shouldst thou stay alone after I have gone up? But I could stand here yet another hour. Thou must go next."

"I will stay to the last," answered Grani. Then the rope came down again. "I will not go," said Grani.

"Then I shall tie thee by force, and send thee up," said Frodi.

But then was heard a great shouting, and there came a ship which had seen the work of rescue, and had put in shore. Grani said: "I will go in the ship; they are sending a boat." When the boat came from the ship, Grani went in it; but Frodi climbed the rope and told Rolf what had been said.

That was a ship of chapmen, and its master asked Grani who he was, and gave him food and drink, and carried him round the end of the Mainland to Hawksness; but those others who had reached the top of the cliff had no other way than to walk. Four leagues they fared on foot, reaching Hawksness after nightfall. Meanwhile Grani spoke much with the shipmaster, and they grew very friendly. They came to Hawksness about the same time as the other men came from the moors, and they all walked up to the hall together.

Rolf walks with Frodi, but the shipmaster goes with Grani, and passes near them; the shipmaster sees them, but they do not mark him. Then the shipmaster pulls at Grani's sleeve, and draws him aside.

The shipmaster asks: "Those two who walk there are thy thralls?"

Grani said so. Then the shipmaster said: "Didst thou say thou wouldst set them free?"

"Aye," answered Grani.

"It hath come to my mind," said the other, "that they did not save thee, but I did. Moreover, there was no need for climbing the cliff, for I should have been able to save ye all."

"That is true," said Grani.

"Now," quoth the shipmaster, "thou art very reckless of thy possessions if thou settest those thralls free."

"Truly," answered Grani, "I will not free them."

When they reached the hall Sweyn had arrived before them, and the booty of the vikings lay in the hall; but Ar was waiting anxiously for his foster-son, and welcomed him gladly. Then a true tale was required of all that had happened.

Grani told each thing as it had come about. When he told of his thralls, Ar said: "Since those two are Icelanders, who are close to us by ties of blood, it were better to have set them free."

"Thou didst not reserve any save Orkneymen," answered Grani. Then he told of the wreck and the rescue.

Said Ar: "So those two have their freedom in the end?"

Grani called Rolf and Frodi to the dais. "Thou didst not save my life," said he.

"That is true," answered Rolf.

"Moreover," quoth Grani, "the ship would have saved us all."

"That also is true," said Rolf.

"Therefore I see no reason," said Grani next, "why I should set thee free."

Rolf and Frodi answered nothing. "See," said Grani to Ar, "they make no objection; therefore I shall keep them as thralls. But I will give each of them what he cares to choose of the spoil, if thou permit."

Then permission was given, and the spoil of the vikings was spread out there before the dais; there were fine things of many kinds. But Rolf put the gold and silver by, and took only a cloak. Then said Grani: "Choose again."

Rolf took a belt.

"Choose again," repeated Grani.

Rolf took a short sword.

"Choose yet again!" cried Grani. But Rolf would take nothing more, and Frodi took naught but a cloak and a whittle. "A strange pair are ye," quoth Grani.

But Ar called them to him and asked them why they had chosen so little.

"We take only our own," answered Rolf.

"Sea-worn cloaks and weapons," said Ar, "are they dear to ye?"

"His mother," said Frodi, "made me my cloak, but the whittle belonged to my father."

"And thy things," asked Ar of Rolf. "Who gave them to thee?"

"Snorri the Priest," answered Rolf, "gave me the cloak, and Burning Flosi gave the belt; but if ye do not know these names—"

"I know them both," said Sweyn the sea-captain. "But who gave the sword?"

"Kari Solmund's son," answered Rolf, "and that name thou shouldst know best of all."

Sweyn cried: "I know the man himself, for he is an Orkneyman by birth, tribute-taker here under Earl Sigurd, and of great fame. Now tell us the story why he gave thee the sword."

But Rolf would tell nothing. Then Sweyn offered to buy Rolf of Grani, but he puffed out his lips and would not sell his thrall. So nothing came of that rescue by Rolf, save to give him a name among the Orkneyingers.

Now all men sit down for the evening meal. That shipmaster wishes to leave the hall, saying he must look to his ship; but Grani will not let him go. Then Frodi sees him, and pushes Rolf in the side. Says Frodi: "Men said your uncle was dead."

"So they did," answers Rolf. But he does not attend, and falls to brooding. So Frodi says that again. Rolf asks him why.

"Who sits by the dais?" asked Frodi.

Rolf looked on that shipmaster, and it was his father's brother, Kiartan.

XX

How Rolf Won His Freedom

NOW WHEN THAT meal was ended, Kiartan rose up and said that he must go; he thanked Ar, and Grani walked with him to the door. But as they passed by the bench whereon Rolf and Frodi were sitting, Grani beckoned them to rise up, and he said to Kiartan: "Look on my thralls, now that thou canst see them closer, and tell me what thou thinkest of them."

Kiartan scarcely looked at them. "They seem a good pair," he answered. "It is fitting for thy dignity to have thralls." Then he went away.

Frodi asked of Rolf: "Did he know us?"

"He knew us well," answered Rolf.

"What wilt thou do?" asked Frodi.

"I see naught to do," said Rolf. "For what he did against my father was done in Iceland, so that I could not bring a suit at law here. Moreover, no thrall can bring a suit in any land."

"Wilt thou claim kinship with him?" Frodi asked.

"Wilt thou?" responded Rolf. No more words were

said, but it was seen in their eyes that for their pride's sake they would make no claim on Kiartan.

Kiartan found that nothing was said in the matter; so he stayed there in the place, and won the friendship of Ar by gifts, and traded with success. He ate often at the hall, and slept there whenever he would; but no word passed between him and those kinsmen, nor did they ever look at him.

Grani was proud that he owned thralls, and he commanded them to show what they could do. So Rolf shot with the bow, and Grani made him his bow-bearer. But Frodi said he knew little of weapons; yet when they gave him a spear he shot it through two shields braced together against posts. He asked for work as a smith, but Grani made him spear-bearer. And the youth often walked abroad with those other two attending him. Ar was pleased with that show, but the thralls smiled grimly to each other.

Once Kiartan saw that smile, and he said to Grani privily: "Thy thralls smile at thy back, and make as if they feel shame. Now be careful lest they harm thee sometime when thou art alone with them. If I were thee, I would set them at the sheep-herding or the field-work."

Grani answered: "I fear no harm from them, and indeed I like them more every day. I cannot spare them."

Now the truth of the matter was this, that Grani cast a great love upon Rolf, and would have him as a friend, not thinking that no friendship can be between master and slave. He gave Rolf gifts, everything but his freedom; he spoke much with Rolf, yet the talk was most upon the one side, for Rolf grew very silent. Yet Rolf went everywhere after Grani, and did him much service of all kinds, being clever with his hands and wise in his ways; he knew a boat and all the modes of fishing; when it came to cliff-climbing, no man in that place was his match. Grani often went seeking adventure with Rolf and Frodi; they managed in such wise that Frodi did the work and Rolf directed what should be done. When they went after birds Frodi sat at the top of the cliff and held the rope, but on the cliff's face Rolf would let Grani take no risks. Nay, sometimes it seemed as if Rolf were the master and Grani the man. But when other people were about, Rolf did all that Grani said.

One day a bishop came to Hawksness and visited the parish. He held service in the church, and lived at the hall for two days. When he was about to go away, he asked if any man needed from him counsel or comfort. Frodi stood up. Said he: "Lord Bishop, are all manslayings sinful?"

The bishop answered: "State me the case, for some manslayings are blameless."

So Frodi spoke thus: "If a man is on a ship, and vikings come, and that man casts a viking overboard, and the viking is drowned—hath the man committed a mortal sin?"

Many men smiled at these words, for the story of Frodi and the vikings had been told. The bishop said: "Vikings are the worst plague of the land, and they deserve no mercy. Since the viking came to take life, it was no sin to slay him."

Frodi drew a long breath, but he asked further: "If two vikings were drowned, what of that?"

"It is the same," answered the bishop.

"But if three men were thus drowned," asked Frodi, "what then?"

"Even if thirty died," answered the bishop, "the answer is still the same."

Then Frodi heaved a great sigh, and looked so relieved that all who stood by shouted with merriment. Grani was pleased most of all, and he gave command that Frodi should be called Drowning-Frodi. Frodi liked that little, yet by that name he was called for a while. And Grani was so pleased with all this that he boasted much about his thralls. One day he spoke of them with Kiartan, and told how when they went away together Rolf took the lead. "And he cares for me," said Grani, "as if I were his brother; but so soon as others are by he is as any other thrall, and says no word unless spoken to."

Kiartan said: "In that he appears to me sly."

"How should that be?" asked Grani.

"He seeks to gain influence over thee," answered Kiartan.

"Nay," said Grani, "he and I are friends."

Kiartan shook his head. Quoth he: "In my country

we have a saying: 'Ill is a thrall for a friend.' More-over, to lack dignity at any time is not seeming in one of thy station."

Grani took those sayings much to heart; he went no more away alone with his thralls, but stayed where were other men. Now that was the time when the summer had passed by and harvests were all in, but winter had not yet come and the weather was mild. Men were saying that when winter should come, it would be with suddenness.

There came a day when the wind was high, but it was as soft as summer. A man named Thord the Weatherwise came to Ar and said: "See to it that all is ready for the winter!" and without more words departed. Ar inquired of his men if the sheep were yet gathered in from the downs above the cliffs. It was answered that they were not. Ar bade send a man quickly to warn the shepherds.

It was told Ar that the fishers had just come in, and that all the serving-men were busied at the beach, being much needed to save the catch of fish, for the waves were high. Ar said to Grani: "Lend me one of thy thralls to take my message."

"Thou mayest have both of them," answered Grani.

So Rolf and Frodi prepared to go to the downs, and a long jaunt that would be. But when Grani saw they were ready he felt desire to go with them, since he had not done much for some days, and needed action. So he said that Rolf and Frodi should wait till he could go with them. They went outside the hall to wait, and Grani bound on his shoes. Now Kiartan had stood by and heard all that, and he said:

"So thou goest out again with thy friends?"

Grani answered with pride: "I go with my thralls!"

He went outside the hall and found Rolf and Frodi waiting. Rolf looked him over, and seeing there was no one by, he said: "Take thy cloak, for we may be benighted."

"Lo," answered Grani, "the thrall gives orders to his master! We shall be back before men go to bed. No cloak is needed, and I forbid ye to take yours."

So Rolf and Frodi left their cloaks behind, and went with Grani to the moors. The moors were wide and rolling, and lay above those cliffs whereby they had once been wrecked. The three travelled not as had been their wont, all together; but Grani went ahead, saying to himself they should remember that they were thralls. In going so he missed his way, and they came to the sheepcotes roundabout and late. There they found the men busy gathering in the sheep, making ready to drive them to the valleys when this gale should pass. Some men said that would be on the morrow, for the wind was falling. Even while they spoke the wind dropped completely, and there was a calm.

"See," said Grani, "the storm is over; it was but a gale."

The head shepherd said he thought not so, and that more was to be looked for. "Moreover, thy Icelanders think the same, as I can see by their faces."

"I ask not what they think," answered Grani. "There is blue sky in the south."

"Thy thralls and I," replied the shepherd, "look to the north. And now I beg that thou wilt stay here overnight, for company's sake."

"I see thou hast fear for me," said Grani. "But I will return."

"Then hasten," begged the shepherd.

But Grani would not hurry, and started leisurely. The shepherd called a man, and privately told him he should guide those three, for he knew the moors. Then the shepherd begged Grani that the man might go to Hawksness with him, for his work at the folds was done. The four started together.

Soon a little wind, thin and keen, began to blow from the north; it grew greater quickly until it was half a gale. By that time they were where they could see the sea, and Grani looked out upon it. Quoth he: "Fog is coming from the water."

Now Rolf had been silent so far, all that afternoon; yet he could be so no longer. Said he: "Not fog is that, but snow, and I beg thee to turn back."

"Lead forward!" said Grani to the shepherd. So they went on as they had been going, another half-hour, and each minute the wind grew stronger. They neared the line of the cliffs, and walked parallel with them at a half-mile's distance. Then that which had appeared to be fog on the water at last moved inland, so that they saw it coming like a wall. It left the sea, and swallowed up the land before it; then it swept upon them silently, and they bent before its onslaught. Wind buffeted them and roared in their ears; a few snowflakes drove along the ground; then they were enfolded in the swirl of snow. All around them became one gray fleece, they could not see for a rod in front, and they shivered with the cold.

They struggled onwards, bending to the wind; and night came down an hour before its time. The snow began to heap thickly, and now it was above the ankle, now a foot in depth; wonderful was that fall of snow. They walked one behind the other, the shepherd in front, then Grani, Rolf, and Frodi, each so close as to touch the next one with his hand. The night grew black, and the wind was loud. Then at last Rolf shouted that they should stop.

"Why sayest thou that?" asked Grani.

"Because I think we near the cliffs," said Rolf.

"I hear no surf," answered Grani.

But the guide thought that Rolf was right. Grani asked what they should do. Rolf answered: "Best stay here till morning."

"Shall I freeze?" asked Grani. "Let us turn away and walk further inland."

"We cannot keep our direction," said Rolf.

"Wilt thou never be silent?" asked Grani. "We will go inland." So they sought to do so, and they walked for another while. Then Grani asked the shepherd if he knew where he was, and the man could not say. When they went on again, Frodi pressed forward and took the place behind the shepherd; and when Grani asked for the place Frodi would not give it. So they walked thus for another while, their feet clogged by the snow, their faces stung with the wind, plodding with great effort and weariness. Then at the end that happened which Rolf had feared.

For of a sudden the roar of the sea burst up at them from their very feet, and the guide, with a cry, sank in the darkness. Frodi clutched at him, but caught only the cloak; the clasp broke, and the man fell to his death. Those other three stood at the edge of the cliff, while below the sea thundered, yet they saw nothing.

Then Rolf took Grani by the arm and drew him away. Frodi followed. The noise of the surf was suddenly lost in the wind, and no one would have known they were near the cliff. Rolf led the way inland, and Frodi walked last; they went very cautiously, and Frodi was ever ready to seize on Grani. At last they reached a mound. In its lee the wind was less, and the snow was piling deep; Rolf scooped space for them all, and there they sat down side by side.

After a space Grani said: "It grows cold." Frodi wrapped him in the guide's cloak. For another while they sat silent, until Grani said again: "I am too weary to walk another step, yet if I sit here I shall freeze. Frodi, what can we do?"

Frodi knew nothing which could be done, "Either we should walk over the cliffs, or die of freezing in the first mile. We must stay here. Take warmth from us."

They sat closer to him, but still he was cold. After a while he said: "I am sorry we brought not our cloaks." They answered nothing. The snow heaped around them, yet Grani fell to shivering. Then he said: "I am sorry we turned not back." They still said nothing. At last Grani could bear it no longer, and he cried:

"Rolf, if thou hast anything to say, say it before we all die!"

Rolf answered: "I have been thinking. What is this mound behind us?"

"There is but one mound on all the heaths," answered Grani. "Men call it the barrow of a viking, who died off the coast, and was buried here with his ship, that he might forever look out upon the sea."

"Then," said Rolf, "there is one thing we can do, and only one, to save our lives; and that is to break into the barrow."

So they fell to digging with their hands at the mound, and they could have done nothing had the earth been frozen. But it was still soft; and they dug until they came to timbers, two feet within the mound. Then Frodi thrust his hands between the timbers, and strained at one, and Rolf and Grani tugged at his waist. The timber broke, and they fell back together in the snow; yet an entrance to the mound was thus made, and when they had enlarged it Rolf went in first, and the others followed.

Within, the air was dead and close; they stayed at the entrance to breathe, yet the place was warmer, and it was a great relief not to feel the wind. But Grani was still all of a shiver, so Rolf went into the mound further, and they heard him stumbling and slipping in the darkness. After a while he came back to them and said: "Here is wood for a fire."

Then they pulled stalks of grass and shook them free of snow; they found in the shepherd's cloak a flint and steel, and so made a fire at the mouth of the barrow. The wind bore the smoke away, and by degrees the air cleared in the mound. Then with brands they went within, and cast the light about.

The mound was made of a viking-ship, a small one, which had been borne there on the shoulders of men. It was propped upright with stones, and roofed over with timbers and planks; dirt had been cast over the whole. They climbed into that ship, and saw by the light of the torches where the old viking sat in the stern. He was in such armor as men had worn long before; he had a helm on his head, and held a sword in his hand, and was very stern of face. There he sat as if he were still alive, but there was no sight in his eyes.

Before him in the ship were precious things of gold and silver, cloths, and weapons. All the oars lay in their places as if ready for men to use them. Very strange was that sight, and those three gazed at it in silence.

"He looks," said Frodi, "as if he would walk."

"Now," said Grani, "I remember the shepherds say he has been seen, and lights have burned at this mound some times of nights. Yet he has never done harm."

"If he is ever to do it, he will do it now," said Rolf. "For he looks as if he mislikes us here."

By that time the place was very smoky from the torches, so they went back again to the entrance and lay down to sleep; they took with them cloths and broidered hangings which had lain by the viking, and with these and the fire they made themselves warm. So, very weary from their walking, they fell asleep.

In the middle of the night Rolf and Grani waked, and missed Frodi from their side. Moreover they heard a noise, which was not the howling of the storm, but was like the splintering of wood and the snarling of men's breaths as they wrestled in fight. Then Rolf snatched a torch from the fire and ran within the mound; Grani followed, and they climbed on board the ship.

There lay Frodi and the viking together: they had been fighting all about the place, and the thwarts and oars were broken; in one place even the bulwark of the ship was torn away. But Frodi had forced the viking into the seat where first he had sat; and there Frodi held him, while the viking struggled still, glaring from glassy eyes, and Frodi could do naught but keep him where he was. Little more breath had Frodi, but yet he held his grip on the viking's arms.

Then Rolf drew his short-sword, and sprang in at the viking, and hewed at the neck of him, so that the head sprang off at the stroke; but no blood followed. Frodi lay and breathed deeply, but Rolf took the head of the viking and laid it at his thigh.

With those heathen ghosts which did harm to men, there was no way to quiet them except to hew off the head and lay it at the thigh. And such things happened to many men, even as is here told; but the greatest ghost-layer, says Sturla the Lawman, was Grettir the Strong.

When Frodi had got his breath, they asked him how all that had come about. "Nothing do I know about it," answered Frodi, "save that he came and dragged me in my sleep hither, and sought to throttle me. I had much ado to master him."

They went back and slept until the day came, but the storm was still so violent that they could not travel. Then they made larger the entrance to the mound so that light came into the ship; and they buried the viking in the ground. Now when they came to examine his treasures, Grani and Frodi were busy long, casting aside each thing for something better. But after Rolf had searched for only a short while, he sat still and looked no further. Grani saw that he had something.

"What precious thing hast thou there?" asked he.

"This," said Rolf, "which I found on the back of the viking's seat."

He showed them a bow which had hung there in a leathern case. Of some foreign wood it was, tipped with horn, and bound at the middle with wire of fine gold to form a grip. It seemed very strong, cunningly made: a wonderful weapon. And there was a quiver with it, bearing thirty arrows, long and barbed for war.

"Now," said Grani, "this is far better than jewels or fine cloths, and it is the best weapon here. Thou shalt give it to me."

Rolf gave him the bow. And when they went again to look out upon the storm, the clouds were breaking and sunbeams were coming through. So they took the bow and some small gear, and started for Hawksness, where they found Ar nigh wild for fear; but their coming made him happy. And Grani told all that had happened to them.

Said Ar: "Methinks thy thralls have saved thy life."

"That is true," answered Grani.

"What wilt thou give them?" asked Ar.

"Whatever they wish," answered Grani. He called on Rolf to say what gift he would like at his hands.

"That bow and those arrows," said Rolf.

"Now," asked Grani, "which is dearest to thee, that bow, or thy freedom and Frodi's?"

"Our freedom," answered Rolf.

"Your freedom shall you have," said Grani. Then, before all who were in the hall, he spoke Rolf and Frodi free.

XXI

How Rolf Won the Viking's Bow

GRANI SENT MEN to the viking's mound, and they fetched home all the precious things which were there, whether gold, silver, cloths or weapons. Among these last was the viking's bill. That was a notable weapon, having a curving blade with a hook springing from its back, and set like a great spearhead upon a pole as high as a man's shoulder. Grani kept all weapons; but he gave Rolf and Frodi things to the value of some hundreds in silver, and begged that they should remain with him in the hall of Ar the Peacock. Yet Rolf bore himself as if he expected more from Grani than gold and silver, and said he could not stay in the hall. Grani complained of that to Ar.

Ar asked: "Knowest thou not what he will have of thee?"

Said Grani, "The bow, belike."

"Not so," answered Ar.

"Well," Grani said, "I will make amends to him by pressing him again to live here with us."

"Thou shalt never succeed with him in that," replied Ar, "until thou hast said those words which will make him forget that he was once a thrall in this place. But this I beg thee, drive him not away from Hawksness; for war with the Scots is threatened in the spring, and all fighting-men will be of value."

So Grani did not press Rolf to stay in the hall, and he asked: "Where will ye live?"

"We go," answered Rolf, "to stay a while with that shipmaster who has been living here."

But when they searched after Kiartan, it was told that he had gone with his ship with great suddenness when he learned that Rolf and Frodi were set free. Yet in his haste he had left merchandise, and had outstanding credits; so Rolf took Kiartan's lodgings, and said he would wait his return. Then winter came on, and the place was snowed and frozen up, so that men had nothing to do save to hold sports on the ice, or to sit long of evenings in the hall, talking of many things. But now all was different from before, and Rolf and Grani came seldom together.

One time when all were at games on the ice, Grani sent for his bow, and it was brought out to him. Men took it and handled it, admiring it much. "Let us see," said Grani, "what shooting we can do with it." He tried to string the bow.

But it was with him as it had been with Rolf and the bow of Grettir: it would not bend for him, but was almost as stiff as a spear shaft. He got red in the face, first with trying and then with anger; at last he gave over and said that others should try. But though the strongest of the Orkneyingers did their best, they could do no better than Grani. Thereat he felt better, and offered the bow to Frodi.

Frodi held it in his hands, and turned it this way and that. "Break it I might," quoth he, "but string it never." He offered the bow to Rolf, saying: "Do thou try it, for I have seen thee do with skill what others have failed to do with force."

But Rolf would not try to string the bow. So Grani sent it back to the hall, and let bring the viking's bill, which had lain by his side in the ship. But when it was brought, it proved too heavy for any of the Orkneyingers to wield.

Then said Grani: "I will give the bill as a present to Ghost-Frodi."

"Why callest thou me that?" asked Frodi.

Grani only said, "Why should I not call thee so?" and he pressed the bill on Frodi, who drew back.

"I know nothing of weapons," said he. Then all the Orkneyingers shouted to see the strongest man drawing away from the bill; and when Grani made him take it, they laughed the more, for he handled it, said all, as if it were the smithy broom. They called him Ghost-Frodi after that, thinking it fine that he who could master a spirit could not handle a weapon.

Now in that winter Ar was continually sick with little fevers, and he would not let Grani stir far from his side. One day a messenger from Earl Brusi came to say that Ar should keep a watch for Vemund the Pitiless, who had been driven from the north, and had gone toward the south. Now no one needed to be told who Vemund was.

For he was the worst of all vikings who had ravaged in the Orkneys, since he not only took tribute, but burnt towns and slaughtered people wantonly. A baresark he was, with the strength of seven men, and so defended by magic that on him no steel might bite. Only twenty men had he with him, but they had the power of fifty, being baresarks all, outlawed and reckless of life. They had first done great damage in Norway, but were driven thence to the Shetland Isles, and thence to the northern Orkneys, but now were coming further south. Rewards and fame were sure to the men who could overcome those baresarks.

Grani begged of Ar that he might go in the warship in search of them; but Ar said no to that. Ar gave orders that Sweyn should keep the ship in readiness; men slept near the boat-stand, ready to launch her day or night.

One night in a storm, fire was seen on that island which is off Hawksness, where dwell only fisher-folk; the cottages were seen to burn to the ground, but the sea was high, and no one crossed over. In the morning a ten-oared boat left that little island, and went away eastward; that was a venturesome thing in a storm, and by that deed that was known for the boat of Vemund the Pitiless. Then Sweyn let launch the

war-ship, and with all his men went after the baresarks. Rolf made no offer to go, and Grani watched
the chase from the shore, angry that he must stay.
The two ships drove away out of sight, and no one
could say that the larger gained upon the smaller.
Nothing more was seen of them all that day.

But in the night the baresarks gave Sweyn the
slip; they came straight back as they had gone, but
Sweyn went on, first east, then south, searching the
coast. Vemund's ship came to Hawksness; and in
the morning, behold, there it was off the landing,
and the baresarks were just rowing it to shore. The
fisher-folk left their cottages and ran to the hall,
and all took hasty counsel. But when word was
brought to Ar of the baresarks, first he became red
in the face, and then he lost power of speech, and
there was no leader save Grani.

Grani said: "This is no place for us to stay, for the
baresarks will burn us alive. Take Ar and the women
and children into the stone church, and let us men
go also thither and defend it." Then that was done;
and when they reached the church, going hastily and
in a body so that none should be left behind, they
found Rolf and Frodi sitting at the door, with their
weapons.

Then all went within the church, but Rolf and
Frodi stayed outside. "Come ye not inside?" asked
Grani.

"All those riches which Ar has in his hall," responded Rolf, "are those to be burned or lost?"

Then Grani said he would go back again, and called for men to help defend the hall. Only nine came. But those, with Rolf and Frodi, went back to the hall; both the hall and the church were barred against the baresarks. Those outlaws came up into the place; a strange crew they were, wearing no armor but skins of beasts, and wild to look on. They burned some huts, but the church and the hall they might not force. Then, because they feared Sweyn's return, and so dared not to lose time, they knew not what to do. Men shot at them from the hall and the church; so the baresarks went back again to the shore, and took counsel together.

Now all the time in the hall Frodi had walked up and down, looking very white and knocking his bill against everything, as if he were afraid. So when the outlaws went away, Grani scoffed at him.

"What dost thou with that bill," asked Grani, "if thou canst not stand up like a man, and be ready for what comes?"

"Truly," answered Frodi, "I feel strange inwardly, and my hands are cold. Yet what dost thou with that bow, which is so handsome that man never saw finer, yet which no one in these islands has yet strung?"

Then Grani took the quiver from his shoulders and laid down the bow. "I am justly rebuked," said he. He took a lighter bow. "Now wilt thou take a smaller weapon?"

"No man can say," answered Frodi, "what he will do in time of trial. But I will keep the bill."

Now some voice was heard without, calling; they listened to what was said. That was a messenger from Vemund, who made this offer: a champion should be sent out by the Orkneyingers, to meet Vemund, and whichever champion should fall, his side should yield itself into the other's hands. But if the Orkneyingers refused, fire should be set to the hall and also to the roof of the church. And that was the same as offering them one small chance for their lives.

Grani asked: "What man will go out against Vemund?"

No one offered. Then Grani said: "He who goes against the baresark will die swiftest, therefore I am willing to go myself."

All the Orkneyingers cried out against that, saying they should die together within the hall; it might be Sweyn would come in time to save them.

Then Rolf spoke and said: "No man in this place, not even Frodi our strongest, will have any chance against Vemund, so long as we fight with steel weapons. For I have heard the ways of such men to be these: before fighting they look upon the weapons of the other champion, and when they look, by witchcraft they make steel or iron powerless against them. Such a man is Vemund named. Yet if thou, Grani, wilt give me what I desire, I will find a way to slay him."

"Anything I have," answered Grani, "is thine."

"Give me then," said Rolf, "the bow and arrows of the viking."

Then Grani gave him the bow and the quiver, and Rolf cried to the messenger to say to Vemund that in half an hour one would meet him with the bow. At that great laughter rose among the outlaws, and those in the hall and in the church felt no confidence in Rolf.

But he said to Frodi, "Go to the forge and heat it." And he said to Grani, "Bring me here some silver." Then when the forge was heated and the silver was brought, Rolf said to Frodi:

"Make me now three silver arrow-heads, the best thou canst, after the pattern of these here in the quiver." So Frodi made the arrow-heads quickly and with great skill, so that no one could have told them apart from the arrow-heads of iron, for they were black from the fire. And Rolf first set a dish of whale-oil to heat by the forge, and then took the heads from three of the arrows. When the new arrow-heads were made, Rolf bound them with sinews upon the shafts.

A man said: "But what wilt thou do with the arrows if thou canst not string the bow?"

Rolf answered nothing. He took the whale-oil and oiled those three arrows. Then he heated the oil hotter, and began to rub it on the bow. First he oiled the string and rubbed it long; then he oiled the wood. And the wood became darker with the oil, and took a finer polish; fresher it seemed, gleaming in the light of the forge. Rolf rubbed for many minutes, and the bow became even darker; he held it then over the forge, turning it in every way, and it took to itself the fire of the coals. Then Rolf oiled the string once more, heating it as well; and at last they saw he meant to string the bow. Against his foot he set it, and bent it, and slipped the string up to the notch; it seemed as if a child could have done the deed, and the men burst out with a shout.

Then Rolf took one of the old arrows and set it on the string; he drew the bow and shot the arrow along the hall. No one could see that it dropped in its flight; but it struck an oaken beam by the high seat, and when men came to measure it afterward, the arrow had entered the oak by the breadth of a palm.

Men spoke afterward of the sweet twang of that bow, like as if it were a harp.

Then the Orkneyingers went out of the hall with much shouting, and stood upon a knoll which was between the hall and the church. The baresarks came near, and Vemund stood out before them; he was a huge man, very hairy, with a great beard. He asked who was to come against him.

"I," answered Rolf.

Vemund laughed, and the other baresarks also, calling Rolf a boy. "Let me see thy weapons," said Vemund. Rolf showed him his quiver, and the baresark touched the point of each arrow with his finger. "Wilt thou look upon my weapons?" asked Vemund.

Rolf said he would not. "Now," said he, "withdraw thy men to the beach, and let us begin."

"Thou art eager for death," said Vemund with a grin. "I will do as thou sayest, and then will come at thee. Thou mayest shoot as soon as thou wilt."

Vemund withdrew his men to the beach, and the Orkneyingers went aside from the knoll. Frodi wept before he left Rolf, commending him to God. Then Rolf took those three arrows with silver points, and stuck them in the ground by his feet.

By then Vemund was ready to return; he bore no shield nor armor; he threw down his bow, and shouted that this should be between whatever weapons each man chose. Then with sword in hand he began to walk to the knoll. Rolf took an arrow from his quiver and laid it on the string.

When Vemund was nearer, Rolf drew the bow; no bow had ever drawn harder, yet none had been so lively in his hand. The arrow sped; Vemund turned not aside, but when the shaft struck on his breast the wood flew to splinters, and the point fell down. All the Orkneymen cried out in fear, but the baresarks shouted. Rolf took a second arrow and waited a while.

Then he shot again, and the arrow struck Vemund on the throat; it turned aside, and flew sliddering away. Some of the Orkneymen withdrew to the door of the church, crying that they should be let in. But the outlaws began to come forward.

Then Rolf drew one of those arrows from the ground, and wiped the point, and made ready.

When Vemund was twenty paces away Rolf shot

for the third time. The arrow went in a level flight, and struck Vemund on the breast; there it sunk to the feathers. Those baresarks, coming behind, saw a foot of the shaft stand out from Vemund's back.

Then Vemund brandished his sword and ran at Rolf; Rolf took the second arrow and sent it at him. In the eye it struck him, and pierced to the brain; down fell the baresark, and died before he reached the ground.

Rolf took the third arrow and put it in his quiver.

Then the Orkneyingers came running from the church with their weapons, and all rushed at the outlaws. Grani shouted that the baresarks should lay down their arms; but they, fearing death, drew into a circle and would not yield. They began to cast spears at the Orkneyingers.

"Shoot arrows at them," said Grani to Rolf.

"I have done my share," quoth he.

Then the Orkneyingers ran round that circle of outlaws, and did their best to pry into it; but they got only wounds. The baresarks began to grit their teeth and work themselves to anger as if they had been wolves; that was their way in battle. Frodi went nearer to look at that sight.

Then one baresark shot a spear at Frodi, and cut his shoulder so that it bled. At that Frodi turned red, and took his bill, and went at that man. The baresark swung his sword, but Frodi caught it with the bill and spun it aloft; then he hooked at the man with the back of the bill, and caught him by the neck, and pulled him down grovelling. An Orkney-man pierced the outlaw as he lay.

So the circle of the baresarks was broken, but they sought to draw again together. Then Frodi took his bill, and made at the two men to right and left of the opening; one he caught with the point of the bill, and pitched him sideways; that man fell on the circle at another place and broke it there. Next Frodi pitched the other baresark clean across the circle against the men at the other side; two fell at once.

Then Grani shouted and rushed within the ring, and all the Orkneyingers fell on the baresarks at every point. Some were slain right there; some broke away and were chased about; one by one they died among the huts and the frames for drying fish.

Frodi, when he had done that much, stood by Rolf and struck no more. When the fighting was finished the Orkneyingers looked to their hurts, and it was found that no one was badly wounded. All said that the death of Vemund the Pitiless was not so bad by half as the living of him.

Now Grani was very happy and talkative, and he praised his men much; but he seemed constrained before Rolf, and spoke to Frodi. "And thou saidst thou couldst not use the bill!"

Frodi answered, "So I thought, but it is no different from handling a pitchfork."

Grani whooped with laughter, and would tell that saying to others. Frodi beseeched him: "Cease thy talking, lest men give me a new nickname."

But Grani told Frodi's words in the presence of many, and all cried that Frodi should be called Pitchfork Frodi. He grumbled to Rolf thereat.

"Better be glad," said Rolf, "that nothing worse has come to thee than a sore shoulder and a new name."

Now Sweyn came sailing back, angered that he had been tricked, but much afraid of what might have happened at Hawksness in his absence. As for Ar the Peacock, he lay without speech until the morrow, when he came to himself; but he was a broken man ever after that shock.

Grani took the spoil from the baresark ship, and divided it into five parts. Two parts he gave to those fishers whose houses the baresarks had burned; one part he divided among those who had wounds; the rest he sent to the lodging of Rolf and Frodi. Grani took nothing for himself, nor did he go with the treasure to Rolf; and men said among themselves that, during all these doings, Rolf and Grani had spoken to each other only when they must.

From that time the viking's bow was Rolf's own. Those two arrows which had slain the baresark were hung up in the church; but Rolf took the third arrow with the silver point, and bound it in the quiver with a silken thread.

XXII

Now Kiartan Returns

AS WEAKNESS grew on him, Ar the Peacock kept Grani much by his side. One day Ar said: "I see that thou art troubled at times. Is aught weighing on thee?"

Grani answered: "Rolf is on my mind."

Ar said: "Put away the thought of him."

"That I cannot do," replied Grani, "for I feel I did wrong in enthralling him, and I cannot be easy until he hath forgiven me."

"Meseems," quoth Ar, "that thou expectest Rolf to come and say 'I forgive thee,' before ever thou hast shown him that thou art sorry."

Grani answered nothing.

"Go now," said Ar, "and seek him out. Confess thyself in the wrong."

"It is hard to do that," responded Grani.

"Thou art well named Grani the Proud," said Ar; but then he added: "Never have I blamed thee till now, but thou shouldst have done this thing at the very first. And the longer this estrangement lasts, the harder it will be to forget."

Grani made no answer, but communed for a while with himself; though it was hard to his pride, at last he decided to humble himself before Rolf. He went to the dwelling of Rolf and Frodi; they were on the headland watching the fishing fleet, and thither Grani followed. He sat down at the edge of the cliff beside those two, and had speech with Frodi; but between him and Rolf passed at the first only the good-day.

Frodi asked: "War with the Scots is expected in the spring?"

"Aye," answered Grani.

"I would I were in Iceland!" Frodi said.

"Oh ye Icelanders!" cried Grani. "Why is it ye always burn to return—whether ye love your foggy isle and plain men more, or our realm less?"

"In your realm," answered Frodi, "there are three pests which no Icelander can bear. The first is your baresarks, which in Iceland are held in restraint, but here they go at large. The second is your vikings, which dare not come to us, but here they harry the coasts. And the third is the habit of burning a man in his house, which by us has been done some few times in great matters, yet is always punished; but here it is done in any little quarrel, and little shame is felt for it. And if I leave this land without being burned, then I am lucky."

Grani laughed, and then Rolf spoke. Quoth he: "And as for our land of simple men against thy realm of kings and earls, all I know is that with us there is law to restrain all men. But if thy earls fall out, then the Orkneys are rent with war. And at all times your lives lie in the power of the Scots, who any summer day may come and sweep the land. Nay, the winter is open: why may they not fall upon us now?"

"It is possible," said Frodi, but Grani had nothing to reply.

"And consider this," Rolf said. "Thou art Grani, fosterling of Ar the thane; thou hast honor, and a part of all spoils are thine. But Ar is coming to his end, and some day another thane will rule here. When thy honors fall away, and thou must take thy place like other men: how then wilt thou think of the doings of kings and earls?"

"I fear no misfortune," answered Grani.

"Then," quoth Rolf, "thou art fitted to be an Icelander. And now I wilt say what I have many times thought: that thy speech is more of Iceland than of this place. Whence did Ar take thee?"

Grani grew red, but answered: "Thou hidest thy parentage."

"True," replied Rolf. "Now I crave thy pardon for questioning thee."

That was the end of that talk, for Rolf drew within himself, and Grani felt shame that he could not ask pardon so easily as the Icelander; and the more he looked on Rolf's countenance the more it seemed that they should be friends. He ceased speaking, and sat with his back half turned, trying to say the words; but for a long time they would not come. At length he said:

"Rolf."

"Aye?" Rolf answered.

Grani said nothing for a while more; at length again he said, "Rolf."

"What is it?" Rolf asked.

But for a second time Grani could not bring himself to speak. Yet at last he made ready to speak without fail and ask forgiveness, and the words were on his tongue.

Then suddenly Rolf rose, and pointed out upon the water, where a ship had come into view; and he cried, "At last cometh he for whom I have waited!"

No need to ask whose ship that was, for Grani saw that it was Kiartan's. And weakly he put aside the chance to set himself right with Rolf, and inquired instead why Rolf waited there for Kiartan so long.

"Tell me first," responded Rolf, "why he cometh in such haste, with oars and sails both. He thinks that by this time I am surely gone; but his debts and goods will not flee from him, and he hath hours before sunset to make the harbor. Can he be pursued by aught? Let us watch the headland to the eastward."

"There comes another ship," cried Frodi.

They watched that ship appear: a war-ship, long and low. Grani cried that that must be a viking, and was for running to the hall; but Rolf bade him wait. Then there came a second war-ship, and two more together, and then a great ship, very large; after that the nose of yet another vessel pushed around the headland.

"Is Earl Thorfinn," asked Grani, "coming to visit his realm?"

"Why should Kiartan," responded Rolf, "flee before the Earl, who hath sold him permission to trade here? That is the fleet of the Scots!"

"More of them are in sight," said Frodi.

So they stayed only long enough to see that the fisher fleet, leaving nets and lines, was hurrying to the shore. Those three left the headland and ran to Hawksness; there they told the tidings and gathered men, arming all those who came to the hall. The women were sent into the church with the children, but the men went down to the beach. There the fishermen first made a landing, and hurried for their arms; but when all were gathered together they were very few against what must be the might of the Scots.

Then the ship of Kiartan neared the shore. Frodi said to Rolf: "Before the Scots come there will be time to claim thy due of him."

"Not in the face of this danger," answered Rolf.

Kiartan ran his ship upon the beach, and his men leaped out and pushed her higher up the shingle. Kiartan ran to Ar, and begged protection. "Fight thou with us," quoth Ar. "We shall be but six score against six hundred." Kiartan turned pale and bit his fingers.

Frodi said, "He is as big a coward as I." Grani laughed.

Now when the Scots neared the shore, the people gave way from the beach and drew a little up the hillside; and the nearer the Scots came, the more the Orkneymen withdrew. Then when the Scots were landing, some of the Hawksness men threw away their arms and sat down where they were; and some fled away to the downs and the heather, where they might hide. But Ar said he would not flee, and went back again to fight. Those who went with him were only Grani and Sweyn, and Rolf and Frodi followed behind.

"This is no Icelander's quarrel," said Ar. "We go to die, but the Scots will give you peace."

"Nevertheless we will look on a while," answered Rolf.

Then Ar took his stand on that knoll whence Rolf had slain the baresark; he had his church and his hall at his back, and thinking to die as became a man he seemed to gain his strength again, and shot arrows in marvellous wise. Twenty he sent among the Scots as they landed, and hurt a man with each; then he took his spear, and waited for the Scots to come nearer.

"Now," said Frodi to Rolf, "shall we stay or go?"

"If we stay," answered Rolf, "we never see Iceland again. Yet I have not the heart to leave those three as they stand there." So he and Frodi drew still nearer to Ar, and stood at his back.

But some archer in the fleet sent forth a shaft, and it smote Ar; in the throat it smote him, and he fell.

Like a man he died there, near his father's hall; and the Scots, shouting, began to come forward. "Flee!" said Sweyn to Grani.

"Wilt thou flee?" asked Grani.

A spear struck Sweyn in the leg, and down he sat. "Here I stay," quoth he.

"Then here stay I," answered Grani.

But those fisher-folk who had thrown down their arms ran to Grani in a crowd, and cried that he should not stay to be killed. Some bore Sweyn within the church, where no Scot would slay him before the altar; and when Grani saw that, he suffered himself to be pushed away. So he came to the hillside before ever the Scots reached him; and when they began to shoot at him with arrows, he ran. And Rolf and Frodi ran along the hillside a little higher up.

Now the Scots sent swift archers in chase. Grani was armed and had heavy weapons; Frodi was slow and Rolf would not leave him; so the archers began to come up on them, and it looked bad for them. Grani knew the country; he sought the best ways, calling to Rolf that they should meet at the Vale of the Hermit. Then he threw off his mail and ran freely, and shook off his pursuers in a little wood. But in that same wood Rolf took the wrong course; for thinking he knew the way to the Vale he led Frodi where should be a glen with a growth of trees.—Nothing was there of the kind, but a bare hillside rose, where was no cover, and the Scots began to shout as they saw them close in front.

Now Grani knew the way better. When he reached the copse he stood and looked where Rolf and Frodi ran on the hillside above him. Then he heard a panting, and looked down. There was Kiartan hiding in the fern.

"Look up now," said Grani, "and see who runneth there above us."

When Kiartan saw Rolf, first he started and then he looked sidewise at Grani. "They can never escape," said he.

"I will call them hither," replied Grani.

"That will bring us in danger!" Kiartan cried.

But Grani leaped upon a boulder and prepared to shout. Then as he stood there, Kiartan snatched up a billet of wood and smote at him from the side: foul was that assault. The stroke fell on the shoulder, but Grani twisted his arm and cast the billet aside; he smote in return, and Kiartan fell. So Grani shouted aloud to Rolf, who stood on the hillside with Frodi and studied his road.

So many copses did Rolf see that he knew not where to go, for most were but small clumps, where was no safety; and only one led to the hidden winding water-course and the secluded dell. But when he heard Grani and saw him, he turned thither, although he must go back a little way. He and Frodi ran hastily, rushing down the hillside with much speed. And they saw they could avoid all but one of the Scots.

That man had run wide of their track, flanking them lest they should double back; now he ran in on them and prepared to strike with his sword. On that slope was no good footing; but the Scot braced himself where the Icelanders must pass, and they could hardly both escape him without a wound. But when Rolf rushed down on him, with sword raised, and those two looked into each other's eyes, then the Scot did not strike, but stood like stone. Neither did Rolf smite, but Frodi struck hard with the butt of his bill; they left that Scot lying in a heap, and sped downward into the hollow.

There they found Grani with Kiartan, and Grani had bound the shipmaster's hands behind his back. Hastily they went into the copse, driving Kiartan before them; they found the crooked water-course and followed it among the stones; it was dry and they wet not their feet. So in a while they came to a little dell, nestled among the hills; the place was called the Vale of the Hermit. But no one lived there, only in one place had been a farm; the hall had been burned, but a storehouse still stood stout against the weather. Thither they went and rested, knowing that no Scot could find them in that place.

Grani loosed Kiartan and bade him gather wood. "And if thou seekest to flee thou wilt carry an arrow in the ribs. Make a fire, for I see beef is in the storehouse, drying, and the green hide hangs against the wall. We will sup." So Kiartan gathered wood and made a fire.

"One thing I fail to understand," said Frodi to

Rolf: "why neither thou nor that Scot smote at the other, and it was left to me to knock him down."

"That was strange to me also," said Grani.

Rolf said: "I knew that man, and he was Malcolm, my father's thrall. For very astonishment we could not strike."

"Then I gave him a headache," quoth Frodi, "to make him remember his manner of gaining his freedom."

"Preserve me from such headaches as thou dealest!" said Rolf. "The butt of thy bill is worse than the point."

Then Grani told why he had bound Kiartan. "And now," said he, "thou canst take on him thy vengeance, whatever that may be."

"Call him here," said Rolf.

So Kiartan was called thither and crouched thereby; it was plain that he expected to be killed. "In what has he offended thee?" asked Grani.

"Now," answered Rolf, "that which I say in his hearing will be to him the worst part of his punishment. He is my uncle, and through him my father came to his death."

But when they looked to see him weep, or hear him blame himself, Kiartan rose and thanked them that his life was spared. In loathing they bade him go into the storehouse and lie; then they laid themselves down inside the door, and slept.

For the sake of air, they left the door wide. In the

morning they found that Kiartan was gone; and while they were asking where he might be, they heard his voice at a little distance, saying that there those three lay in that storehouse, and the Scots should slay them. Then was heard the rush of feet.

XXIII

Of the Coming of Earl Thorfinn

ROLF SHUT THE storehouse door, and Frodi held it until it was barred. The Scots could move neither Frodi nor the bars, and knew not what to do. All within was dark, save for light from the crack of the door; and when the Scots who stood before the crack felt Frodi's bill, they stood back. Then Rolf shot arrows out through the crack, and the Scots stood aside, so that those within could do no more. They heard the Scots say that no time should be wasted for three men.

"Now," said Frodi, "they will go away."

"Be not too hopeful," said Grani.

When smoke began to puff in, they knew that the thatch had been fired over their heads. "So," quoth Frodi, "I shall be burned in the Orkneys after all. Seest thou, Grani, why no Icelander loves thy land?"

They sat there a while and the place grew hot; then Grani began to pace up and down. "Would that I," he said at last, "had never seen the Orkneys!"

"What is this?" asked Rolf.

Grani said after a silence: "I shall never speak

again to my father, whom I have not seen these many years." Next he said: "My sister must be almost a woman." After that said he: "Peaceful was our home."

Frodi tried to comfort him, but Grani would not listen. "Let us die in the open," he cried, "and give an account of ourselves!"

But when they tried to leave that smothering place, they found the Scots had braced the door, and it could not be moved. Then a corner of the roof fell down, and burned inside the storehouse.

"Now," cried Grani in despair, "would I were once more on the home-field of Fellstead, looking abroad on old Broadfirth and the peaceful dales!"

"A wonderful thing thou sayest!" exclaimed Rolf.

"Let wonders be," said Frodi. "But since we cannot leave this place by the front door, why not by the rear?"

"How do that?" asked Grani.

Frodi drew aside the heavy hide which hung at the back of the storehouse, against the rock of the hillside: there were a carved stone doorway and a black cave.

"Now," cried Grani, "rightly is this place called the Vale of the Hermit; this was his house, though I never knew of it till now. Let us be quick!"

So they went into that cave and sat there, while the fire burned the storehouse quite away, and its roof-beams fell across the door of the cave and hit it. Moreover the green hide did not burn through, and kept out the smoke; and a little air came in through a fissure of the rock. Then the Scots who watched went their way, and Kiartan with them. When they were gone, those three thrust the hide and the beams aside from the cavemouth, and leaped out over the embers. They were near stifled, and weak from the heat.

Those Scots and Kiartan went back to Hawksness, and for what he had done they gave him his ship unplundered. But they plundered the hall and the church, and with the riches of Ar they had both sport and quarrels, until all was divided. Then they sent out vessels to ravage in the Orkneys; but the main body, and the leader, sat there at Hawksness, and because it was believed Earl Thorfinn thought them still in Scotland, and no ship had been spared to go south and tell of them, they had no fear of him. For it would have been a great undertaking for any small boat to cross the Pentland Firth.

But on a day when the Earl sat in his hall, in Thurso of Caithness, his men came to him, saying: "There are messengers without, and they would speak with thee." But the men laughed.

"Why laugh ye?" asked the Earl.

"The messengers say they are from the Orkneys, yet no ship has come, and they are the worst of scarecrows."

"But bring them in," said the Earl.

So three men were brought before the Earl. One was of middle height, and slender; he bore a bow.

One was taller, and carried a sword. The third was as big as any man in that place, and he held in his hand a great bill. All in rags were those men, as if their garments had been scorched. They told the Earl that the Scots were in the Orkneys, and the Earl's men laughed mightily.

"Sailed ye across the Firth?" asked the Earl.

"We rowed," answered they.

"In what?" asked the Earl. "And where is the boat?"

"It sunk off the shore," said those men, "and we swam the last mile."

"Why are ye so burned?"

They said they had been nigh burned to death.

Then the Earl stilled the laughter of his men, and he leaned to that one who bore the bow; he was not much more than a lad. "Where didst thou get," asked the Earl, "that short-sword which thou wearest? For I know the weapon well, since once it belonged to Earl Sigurd my father."

"That may be so," said the lad, "but it was given me out in Iceland."

"Now," said the Earl, "I know the man to whom my father gave the sword, and he went out to Iceland. Tell me what man gave it thee; if the name is the same, then will I believe this news of thine. But if the name is different, then ye three shall die for your false word."

"A light matter on which to hang lives," quoth

that one. "Who knows how many have owned this sword? But I got it from Kari, Solmund's son."

The Earl smote his thigh. "And to Kari my father gave it! Up, men, and dight yourselves for war! This day we sail for the Orkneys."

So Earl Thorfinn sailed north, and with him went Grani, Rolf, and Frodi, those bearers of the tidings. And before ever the Scots were ready for them the Orkneyingers closed in upon Hawksness, and attacked the Scottish fleet. Some of the Scots were away, and some were ashore; those who might fight lashed their ships in a line, as in a line the Earl's ships bore down on them. That fight lasted not long, and all the Scottish ships were taken; the Scots who were on shore were hunted down, and as their ships came in from the other isles, they were taken one by one.

Kiartan's ship was still on the beach, and he was found in the church.

XXIV

Now Rolf and Grani Quarrel

NOW SAYS THE tale that Rolf goes before the Earl, and tells of Kiartan's treachery.

"Thou shalt have thine own way with him," quoth Thorfinn. "Shall he die by the hands of my men, or what atonement wilt thou take?"

"I ask not his death," said Rolf. "Give me his ship to return to Iceland in, and his goods to repay my mother for all her sufferings." But of those sufferings, nor of all that Kiartan had done, the Earl did not ask until later.

"Thou art easy," said he, "upon him who sought thy life; but all shall be as thou sayest."

Then Grani spoke apart with the Earl, and after that Thorfinn gave orders to his men. Where the sward lay greenest (for no snow lay on southern slopes all that winter) they cut a strip of turf; its middle they raised and propped aloft on spears, but its ends were still in the ground. Then the Earl called Rolf to come, and bade all men stand there and hear what Grani had to say. Before all, Grani

168

told that he had wrongfully enthralled Rolf, and led by Kiartan had treated him unfairly. His sorrow he confessed, and he asked for pardon.

Answered Rolf: "For this I grant pardon readily enough."

"Meseems thou sayest that coldly, man," said the Earl. "Now here stands Grani to swear blood-brothership with thee, under this turf. What sayest thou to that?"

Now blood-brothership was a sacred ceremony, and those who swore it must uphold each other until death, if once the oath was taken under such a strip of turf, by letting blood from the arms mingle in the ground. And no greater honor might one man do another than to offer blood-brothership. But again Rolf spoke coolly, and said:

"Mayhap I am willing to do that."

"Come, then," said Thorfinn. "Lay aside thy sword, and step under the turf with Grani."

"Once I swore," replied Rolf, "never to leave weapon from my reach. And another oath I call to mind, which later I may tell thee here. Now since blood-brothership is asked, here I name myself: Rolf, son of Hiarandi, of Cragness above Broadfirth in Iceland. And remembering what Grani said when we were like to be burnt together, I ask his true name, and his father's name, and his birthplace."

"Grani hight I," answered that one. "Years long have I been fostered here, and I remember little of my childhood. But Einar is my father, Fellstead was our home, and the place is that same Broadfirth out in Iceland. So much I know and no more."

Then those who stood by saw Rolf draw his short-sword and spring at Grani. At his forehead Rolf laid the sword, the flat to the skin. "Thus," cried he, "I laid this sword to thy father's head. But thus" (and he turned the sword) "I lay it to thine, edge to thy flesh. And because I promised to do it, thus I draw thy blood!"

He drew the sword lightly across Grani's fore-head, and the blood started out in little drops. Then Rolf dropped his arm, sheathed his sword, and stood quiet; but Grani, white with rage, snatched a spear from one of the Earl's men, and would have slain Rolf had not the Earl himself come between.

"Now," quoth Thorfinn grimly, "here is an odd end to blood-brothership. The cause of this shall I hear, from first unto last."

Then Rolf told the story of his father's wrongs and his own, and Frodi said it all was true. Grani, though he learned what his father had done, stood still and said no word, except that he cried at the end:

"Great insult hath Rolf offered me in drawing my blood, and for that shall he pay with his."

"Meseems," answered the Earl, "that the weight of blood-debt is still on thy side, and it is well for thee that Rolf took not payment in full. And this I advise, that here ye two make up the feud; and all money atonements I will make to Rolf, if so be I see ye accorded."

"I will lay down the feud on these terms," said Rolf, "if Grani will get me my homestead again."

But deep anger burned in Grani that his offer of blood-brothership had been so answered, by the shedding of his blood. He strode to the spears that held the strip of turf, and cast them down. "My feud do I keep!" he cried.

"Then of thee," said the Earl, "I wash my hands. But I will take Rolf to me, to be of my bodyguard so long as he will."

"Lord Earl," answered Rolf, "I thank thee for the honor, but in the ship which thou hast given me I must return to Iceland, there to clear me of mine outlawry by means of my bow."

And then that meeting of men broke up, and Rolf set himself to fit his ship for the outward voyage, and to hire sailors. He had wealth enough, in Kiartan's goods, to pay for all his father had lost; but in the viking's bow he had that treasure which he most prized, for it should win him his honor again, and the homestead which his fathers had built.

He provisioned his ship, and he hired men and a shipmaster, and soon was ready for the voyage outward. Now the spring was early, without storms as yet.

But Grani went unhappily about, knowing that danger was preparing for his father, through Rolf, and seeing not what could be done. For in that place, except Rolf's ship, lay no vessels plying either north or south, and none to go to Iceland. So there was no way for Grani to send warning to Einar, and no means by which he himself might go to Iceland, to stand by his father's side. He would have challenged Rolf to the holm, but holmgangs and all duels were forbidden by the Earl. And now came the day when Rolf's ship was ready; the wind was fair from the east, and on the morrow they should start. Then Grani went and sat on the hillside at sunset, watching the men at a little distance as they worked about the ship where it lay upon the strand; but Rolf and Frodi had gone to the hall, and were feasting there with the Earl and his men.

Grani thought: "To save my father I must sail on that ship. Now the night will be dark, and the men will sleep at the huts, but Rolf and Frodi at the hall. Naught hinders me from hiding myself on the ship, so that on the morrow they will sail with me."

That pleased him well. But before dark Rolf and Frodi returned from the hall, having said farewell to the Earl.

The ship was then pushed off, and all men got them aboard; they anchored off the boat-steads, ready to sail at first twilight in the morning. Then when Grani saw his plan spoiled, in great uncertainty of mind he went to the hall and sat down on the lowest bench.

Quoth the Earl: "Come forward, Grani, and sit here near the dais; for thou didst save my realm as much as did those other two who have just said farewell."

"I know that well, lord," answered Grani.

"Come, sit here by my side," said the Earl, "and what thou askest in reward for thy deed, that I will give thee."

So Grani sat there by the Earl's side until it was dark out of doors, and he knew the stars were out, but no moon. With the feast, Thorfinn waxed joyous, for good tidings had come that day; and he began to press Grani to name the reward he would have for crossing the Pentland Firth to bring him news. So Grani said:

"Stretch forth thy hand now, Earl Thorfinn, and promise to grant me that thing which I ask, which shall take from no man his right or his own."

So the Earl stretched forth his hand in promise, and said: "Ask what thou wilt."

Then all the Orkneyingers listened while Grani made his request. "Oh Earl," said he, "make me thine outlaw!"

"Nay," cried the Earl, "what request is this? Dost thou mock me and my power!" And his men were angry, and some drew their swords.

But Grani said most earnestly, "I mean no insult, but much lies on it that thou shouldst make me outlaw."

Wroth indeed were the Orkneyingers, and thronged around Grani to slay him; but the Earl signed them to give peace, and sat with his eye on the youth, and thought. Then at last he smiled in his beard, and said:

"Thou art a clever lad, and bold withal. Here I

grant thy desire." And he stretched out his hand and said: "Outlaw do I make thee in all my lands—not to be fed, not to be forwarded, not to be helped or harbored in any need, save only by masters of ships outward bound. I grant thee three days' space to seek shelter, and here I give notice among my men of thy full outlawry."

Then Grani thanked the Earl with all his heart, and went from the hall; after him the Earl's men scoffed, but still the Earl smiled in his beard.

Now that night a small boat rowed to the side of Rolf's ship, and a man climbed aboard, and the boat-men rowed the boat ashore again. One of the ship's men told Rolf, who sent for that one who had thus come aboard. He stood before Rolf in the starlight, wrapped in a cloak. Rolf asked why he came aboard the ship in that manner.

"Outlaw am I," said that one, "and by law thou must give me shelter when it is claimed."

"Good is the law," quoth Rolf, "and once it helped me ere now. But thy voice is muffled in the cloak, man. What is thy name?"

"No-man is my name," answered the muffled man, "and here is my faring money."

Rolf laughed. "No-man's fare costs nothing," said he, and would not take the silver. "Find thyself a place to sleep; thou art welcome here."

So that one found himself a place to sleep, and early in the morning the ship set sail. Now it is said that when the ship was gone the Earl saw Kiartan on the strand bewailing his loss. Thorfinn ordered that Kiartan be set in a galley as rower, and for two years did Kiartan labor at the oar. Then he escaped, and fled away southward; but he became thrall to a chapman, and was a thrall to the end of his days. So now he is out of the story.

But that outlaw who had come on Rolf's ship lay like a log all the first day, while the ship sped westward; and only at night did he rouse to take food. Four days he did thus, while the ship ran before the wind until the Faroe Islands were well astern. Then on a morning the man rose and walked by the rail, and looked upon the sea. Rolf sent for him to come and speak to him, and when the man was face to face with him, behold, it was Grani.

Then Rolf stood and looked on him, and Grani stood fast and looked on Rolf. And Rolf turned away and walked in the stern, but Grani waited in the same place. At last Rolf came back to him and said:

"Only one thing will I ask of thee. Wast thou indeed outlaw of the Earl?"

Grani stretched out his hand and swore to the truth. "Outlaw was I, and the Earl gave me but three days to quit his land."

"Now," said Rolf, "thou art on my ship lawfully, and naught will I do against thee. We will leave it to the fates, which of us shall prosper in this affair."

So Grani was out of danger of his life. Now that east wind lasted until they made Iceland—a quick voyage. And they sailed along the south of the land,

and rounded the western cape, and sailed across the mouth of Faxafirth. But when they would round the cape into Broadfirth the wind freshened, and blew them off the land a day's sail; there they lay when the wind dropped. But then the wind came from the west, and blew them back to the land, and drove them ever faster till there was a high gale. The smallest sail they could set split from the mast, the mast itself went next, and so they came to Broad-firth and drove up it. Night drew near, and the sail-ors were in fear of their lives.

Now Frodi was in great uneasiness, and clung to his place, and looked upon the waters. Sometimes he made as he would speak, and yet he said nothing. Rolf and Grani stayed at opposite sides of the ship, and were steadfast in all danger, though the waves washed over them.

Then Rolf makes his way to Grani, and says he: "Now we near the land, and it is likely that we shall never need more of it than a fathom apiece, for burial. Therefore here I offer thee peace, asking no atonement from thee or thy father, save only my farm again, if we twain get ashore."

Grani looks upon Rolf, and his heart nearly melts; but he makes himself stubborn and drops his eyes. Says he: "This is no time to speak of that."

Rolf clambers back to his place. The moon rises behind broken clouds, and he sees that the ship drives toward cliffs.

XXV

Here Rolf Comes to Cragness

NOW TURNS THE tale to speak of Einar, how
he took possession of Cragness (for he bought
the share of the men of the Quarter); and how Snorri
the Priest sent for Asdis that she should come to him
for the sake of Rolf her son, and wait the three years
of his exile. But Asdis answered the messenger of
Snorri: "I go to our little farm in the upland, where I
can look upon my home. We will see if Einar sends
me away also from that."

So she took what goods she might, and drove the
milch ewe before her, and went to the turf hut in
the upland, there to live alone. Now Einar might
have sent her thence, and Ondott was urgent with
him that he should; but for very shame Einar could
not do that wrong, and that one good deed of his
stood him after in stead, as the saga showeth.

Asdis over-wintered there, and folk brought her
meal; but Snorri sent her much provision and dried
fish, to keep her. Before they went away his men
bought wood and drew it for her, and cut turf for
burning; and on parting they gave her a purse of one

gold-piece and six silver pennies, so Asdis was safe from all want. But no happiness could come to her so long as each day she looked out upon the hall at Cragness, and saw strangers there.

Einar abode in great pride at his new hall, and kept high state, sending to fetch whatever travellers came that way. And when harvest came he had a great feast, with all his house-carles and thralls and bonders and neighbors bidden; notable was the state of that feast.

But Ondott, when all were merry, and those who were bidden were saying that Einar was a great chief, on account of his open-handedness—Ondott let call for bows, and said that all should go down to the boundary. There by the brook he held a mock shoot; and one called himself Rolf and made as if he would shoot to the oak tree, but shot into the brook, and wept, and besought others to shoot for him. The looser sort hooted and thought that sport, and shot toward the oak a little way. Then they cried that Hiarandi was lawfully slain, and Rolf was outlaw.

But the neighbors of the better sort liked that not, and changed their aspect of cheer, and went away early. Einar said to Ondott, "Why didst thou such foolery?"

"That we may know," said Ondott, "who are of thy friends, and who thy ill-wishers. And now we know who are with us."

Einar let himself be pleased with that answer.

So the harvest passed, and winter went by and

spring came on, and early spring without storms. All men looked to their plowing and sowing; and Einar took pleasure in the home-fields at Cragness, which were so fertile. But he disliked the lack of storms, for since he came to Cragness no wealth had come to him from wrecks, which he had counted on as part of his riches. And Einar had no custom to light beacons, but all through that spring he and Ondott looked for storms. Men said that storms must come, and that early farers from overseas might be caught thereby. Then at last that steady wind which had blown from the east first dropped, and then shifted, and blew hard from the west, a great gale. All men housed themselves, and a murky night came on.

Now in the hall at Cragness the old crone Thurid sat by the fire and sang to herself; and Ondott, who was ever prowling to hear what men said, came behind her and listened. She sang:

> "Bad luck and good
> Are both abroad.
> If beacon light
> Be set this night,
> Comes Cragness feud
> To quickest good."

"Hearest thou that?" said Ondott to Einar. He sang the song after her.

Einar asked, "Shall we light the beacon?" For he was easily turned in his purposes.

But Ondott smote the old woman, and cried: "Thou singest otherwise than when thou wert with

Hiarandi. Ill was it with Hiarandi when he made
the beacon, and ill would it be with us!"

He asked if he should thrust the woman from the
house, but Einar had not the heart for that. The old
woman said she would go ere the light came again,
and was silent for an hour.

Now it is said that had Einar lighted the beacon,
good would have come of it; for he who saves life is
minded to continue in right doing.

Then after a while the carline sang again. She
sang:

> "Thy rocks beneath,
>   Men fight with death.
>   Go, see what woe
>   Lies there below!"

Einar hurries his men out into the storm, and
himself after them. Now though the gale continues
the moon is bright at last, and men can see their
way.

On the rocks was a ship, and her timbers were
breaking away from her and driving down into the
cove to the lee. Thither Einar sent most of his men,
to save what they could from the sea, of wood, chests,
cloths, and all merchandise. But he watched from the
cliffs, with Ondott and Hallvard and Hallmund, to
see if men escaped from the fury of the sea. He saw
no living thing at all, until at the last one man came
climbing the cliff toward him. That one had a rope
around his waist; when he reached a shelf of rock he

made the rope fast, and drew on it, and pulled up a long case and a bundle: he cast down the rope again, and drew up weapons, and cast again, and drew up clothes.

"Fishes he," asked Einar, "with a hook on that rope?"

Said Hallvard: "Other men must be below, helping him."

Then that man threw down the rope again, and waited a while, and held the rope securely; it seemed as if a weight were on it. Then another man climbed to his side, a large man, and they two pulled on the rope together, drawing it up. There came into sight what seemed a dead body; but now, where climbing was easier, those two carried the body to the top of the cliffs, and then drew up the case and the arms. Einar and his men went thither in the moonlight, but ere they reached the place the men took the body between them, and carried it to the hall, and into the hall, those others following. Einar went to the door to see what the men would do.

They laid the body down before the fire, and Einar saw it was a handsome youth. Then the men looked about them as they stood; their backs were to Einar, but the crone Thurid saw their faces, and she hobbled up and said "Welcome!"

"There is no welcome for me here," said the shorter of those men, "till these strange hangings are gone from the hall, and it has been purged with the smoke of fire from their contamination."

Now Einar thought he should know that voice. The seafarer said to the crone: "Tell Einar that here lies his son, who comes back to him so; and if the beacon had been lighted, Grani had come in better wise, for I could have beached the ship in the cove. But yet I think he is not dead. And so farewell to Cragness for a space."

So those two turned to the door; and Einar ran forward and cast himself on the body of his son, not looking at those men. But Ondott looked on them, and they were Rolf and Frodi, spent with toil in the water and on the rocks. And when Ondott bade his two men seize them, they were too weary to resist; so they were bound with ropes.

Now Einar saw that Grani was not dead, but stunned by some blow. He called the women and bade them bring cloths, and heat water, and use all craft to bring his son to life again. They set to work, and Helga Grani's sister came and looked on her brother's face for the first time since he had been a little boy.

But Ondott brought before Einar those two, Rolf and Frodi, and said he: "Here we have that ravening outlaw and his cousin; now what is thy will of them? Shall they die here under the knife?"

Einar said: "Nay, but rather set them free."

Ondott cried: "What is thy thought? Here they have come again with designs on thee, and wilt thou let them go? And they will dispossess thy son of his heritage; wilt thou suffer that? Rolf is out of the law, and no harm will come of the slaying."

And Ondott pressed Einar with other reasons, saying that most of their men were at the cove for the jetsam, and Hallmund and Hallvard would never tell.

Now Helga heard, and stood before her father, saying: "Take not this sin on thy head, but rather let both the men go."

Yet Einar's heart was turned to evil as he saw how but two of his men were there, and those of the trustiest; so that those cousins might be quickly slain, and buried, and none would know that they had come ashore from the wreck. "Stand aside," quoth he to Helga, "and let these foes of thy heritage die as they should."

But Helga stepped before Rolf and Frodi, and fronted the drawn swords of Ondott and his men. "Unlawful is such a deed," she cried, "until the morning light comes. For all night-slayings are forbidden, even of outlaws, and such slayings are murder." And when she saw her father waver again she told him how even the Earl of The Orkneys (and he was father of Earl Thorfinn) dared not slay those sons of Njal who came into his hands, and so take the sin of midnight slaying on his soul; but he set them aside till morning should come.

"Aye," answered Ondott, "and in the morning the twain were fled."

That Helga knew, and had the same thought in

her mind; but she begged her father not to take such shame on himself, rather to let Rolf and Frodi lie in bonds till morning. And at last Einar promised her that those two should not die until the day.

Rolf said to her: "I thank thee, maiden; and when I come into mine own again I shall not forget this. For it has been prophesied me that I shall yet sleep in my father's locked bed, and that means that this house shall be mine again."

Then Ondott laughed. "Not so is the prophecy to be read!" he cried. "Throw them into the locked room of Hiarandi for this night. To-morrow they shall sleep soundly elsewhere."

So in that little room where Rolf's fathers had slept he was cast with Frodi, and there they lay on the floor, and had no comfort of that place because of their bonds.

"Now," grumbled Frodi, "vikings have we escaped, and baresarks, and the Scots, and all manner of dangers, and the sea, only to die here at last. What was that foolish tale of thine about a prophecy? I never heard of such a thing."

"Free me of my bonds," answered Rolf, "and thou shalt learn why I made that pretence."

Frodi strove against his bonds, but they were too strong for him; and so those cousins lay there for a while.

But outside in the hall the women worked over Grani until at last he moved and groaned, and they saw that he would live. So for joy Einar knew not

what to do; and he became talkative, and walked
about, and so stumbled on those things (the bundle,
and the clothes, and the arms, and the case) which
had been brought there with Grani. When he examined them the arms pleased him right well, for in
the case he found the marvellous bow of the viking.
All admired the bow.

But the old woman Thurid muttered to herself as
she saw them handling the bow, and at last drew
near and asked to see it. The bow she handled, and
the arrows she looked on; then at last she shuddered
and let the bow fall, and sang of it:

> "Enemy fierce
> To Einar's fame,
> Now lieth here.
> Ere thee it pierce,
> Or bringeth grame,
> Fire it should sear.
> Break it and burn!
> Thus shalt thou turn
> Ill from thy hall,
> Ruin from all.
> —This I discern."

Einar looked with aversion on the bow where it
lay, but Ondott raised it and held it aloft. "Now,"
asked he, "shall such a beautiful weapon be broken
for a crone's rhymes?"

All cried out that it should not be so; and Einar
took the bow, and hung it on his high seat, vowing
to keep it. Then he said to Thurid she should be
gone ere morning, as she had promised. The old

woman took her cloak, and went to the door, but on the threshold she sang:

> "Here got I
> One gray cloak,
> One winter's meat:
> These from Einar
> Here got I.
> —One gray cloak,
> One winter's meat,
> Be given Einar
> Ere he die!"

So she went out into the storm. Now the moon had clouded again, and snow fell thickly, a blinding squall; so the old woman was bewildered, and very cold. She found herself a place by a rock, and sat there, singing verses, until at last she fell asleep.

But while all were admiring the bow in the hall, Helga came to the door of the locked bed, and took away the brace that closed it, and cast in a knife, and shut up the door again. Rolf and Frodi saw; and they conceived this plan, that Rolf should hold the knife in his hands, and Frodi should rub his bonds there against. Then that was done, and they freed themselves.

"Yet we are not out of the hall," said Frodi, "and with helping Grani the place will be awake all night."

"Now remember the prophecy which I coined," answered Rolf. "Look here and hold thy peace."

And he showed Frodi how a panel in the wall might be taken out, so that the way was free.

"Come then," Frodi said.

But Rolf would not. "Why stay we here in danger?" asked Frodi.

"I must have my bow," replied Rolf. "How else shall I win my heritage again?"

But when they tried the door into the passage which led to the hall, it could not be opened without great noise; and ever they heard the women walking about, as they tended on Grani.

"Remember," said Frodi at last, "the choice which Grani once offered thee: the bow or thy freedom. Freedom was then thy choice, and afterward thou didst win the bow. Show now the like wisdom."

So they stole away in the first light of the morning.

XXVI

Of Grani's Pride

IN THE EARLY morning Grani slept quietly at last, and the household of Einar had peace. Then Ondott called Hallvard and Hallmund, and bade them come with him. To the locked bed they went, but though the door was still secure, no sign of those two cousins was to be found, nor any way of their escape. And outside the wind had so drifted the snow that no marks of feet were to be seen. Ondott and his men searched, and came at last to the cove where men watched for the wreckage. He asked if they had seen those two.

Thither had come, said the men, two whom they knew not, bearing between them old Thurid the crone. Now at that hour a spar from the ship had just come ashore, and in it was fixed a great bill, its blade driven so deep into the wood that with all their might three men could not draw it forth; they were about to hew it out with axes. Then the taller of those two men came down to the shingle, and said naught to Einar's men; but he laid hold of the bill and with one tug plucked it forth from the spar, and went off brandishing it and muttering to himself. Next the two took the old crone again, and went away.

Ondott and his men hurried on their track, and when they had passed down into the hollows, there the marks of feet were found, pointing straight to the little hut on the hillside where Asdis dwelt, a league away. So Ondott took more men, and went thither, and knocked on the door. Within were Asdis, and Frodi, and the carline Thurid; but no sign of Rolf was to be seen. Frodi sat by the fire and handled the great bill, and Thurid lay muffled on the floor as she was wont; there was a smell of cooking, while very pleased did Asdis seem.

"Where is thy son?" asked Ondott.

"Find him who can," answered Asdis.

They searched that place and found him not, and there was no room to have hidden a man. So Ondott was angry, and he said to Frodi: "Give us that bill, which is Einar's, since it came ashore on his beaches."

Frodi answered mildly: "I pray thee leave it me." But as he spoke he thrust the butt of the bill down upon the floor, where the earth was tramped as hard as any stone; and the butt made a great dent in the floor. Ondott thought it best not to meddle with him, and went home empty-handed.

Grani lay two days sick and weary, but then he was himself again. Neither Einar nor any of his men told him how he came ashore, but spoke as if they

had saved him. Einar sent men everywhere to find
Rolf and seize him; yet in all the dales no man had
seen or heard of him. So when Grani asked if others
got ashore from the wreck, Einar answered: "That
outlaw Rolf, and his cousin Frodi. And Frodi is at
his smithy again, there not far from the ferry to
Hvamm."

"Where is Rolf?" Grani asked.

"No man knows save Frodi," answered Einar, "and
he sayeth not."

Then spoke Grani, lying on his bed. "Father, Rolf
told a hard tale against thee in the Orkneys: how
thou slewest his father foully, and now holdest his
land in spite of right. Now tell me the truth of all
this, ere I accept aught from thee."

Then Einar was greatly frightened lest Grani
should learn the truth and despise him; he made as
if he were offended, and went away, saying: "And
canst thou think that of me?" But when he was out
of Grani's sight, he sought Ondott in haste, and
asked him what he should do.

Quoth Ondott: "Leave all to me. I will settle this."
So he went to Grani, and Einar with him. Einar said:
"I have brought Ondott to tell the truth, for thou wilt
better believe some one else, speaking in my defence."

Then Ondott told a long tale of Hiarandi, how he
was overbearing and insolent, and preyed on Einar's
crops and cattle. Moreover Hiarandi was a dangerous
and violent man, going always armed, so that one day
when he was in the act of theft and Einar's men were

about to seize him—but Einar had commanded not
to harm him—Hiarandi had so attacked those men
that to save their own lives they had slain him. And
Rolf had no right to the land, being outlawed at the
Althing.

"Now tell me," said Ondott, "when ye twain were
together in Orkney, did not Rolf offer peace if thou
wouldst but get him this homestead again?"

"Twice he did that," answered Grani.

"See now," cried Ondott, "the guile that is in him!"

Then Grani believed all that Ondott had said,
and thought evil of Rolf, and craved his father's pardon. Einar forgave him. And when Grani was well
again Einar showered him with kindnesses, for fearing lest his son should learn evil of him he did all
that he might to earn Grani's love, sparing neither
words, deeds, nor money. Einar gave the finest of
clothes, and horses, and attendants, so that not with
Ar the Peacock had Grani had such state. Wherefore he took to himself such pride as had been his
in the Orkneys.

He went abroad among the Iceland folk, and saw
that they were a simple people, each man living upon
his own farm and dressing in plain clothes, loving
direct speech and homely ways. So Grani missed the
best that was in the people, but thought them mean-
spirited. He dressed always in colored clothes, and
had attendants with him, and expected such respect
from men as he had received when he was Ar's Fostering. Now at Cragness honor was always showed

him; but the neighbors of Einar were to Grani blunt of speech, sometimes biting; and he loved them little, thinking them rough.

Two more matters troubled Grani. For he had little happiness in his sister, who seemed almost always downcast, and as if disappointed in him. And ever deep within his heart lay that love of his for Rolf, nor could he forget their comradeship, nor the dangers they had together borne. He took no great satisfaction, therefore, to be a princeling on his land, but away from it to be treated roughly, and always to have that desire to see his friend again. Yet he never made to himself any confession of fault, believing Rolf in the wrong, both toward himself and toward Einar. So he hardened his heart and increased his outward pride, even while he was ever on the watch for news of Rolf.

Now one day he rode abroad with Ondott and his men, and they came to the hut on the hillside where dwelt Asdis the mother of Rolf. Summer was come; Asdis sat out of doors by the spring combing flax, with Thurid cowled by her side. No welcome gave Asdis to them, but asked their errand.

"To learn whether thou hast news of thy son," Ondott said. Now that was not true, for they came thither by accident, having hunted higher up in the hills. But Grani said nothing, wishing to learn of Rolf.

"Ever thou liest in wait for blood," answered Asdis. "But ask not me for news of Rolf. Rather of

those who have been near the isle of Drangey
shouldst thou inquire, if none resembling my son
have been seen on the island-top; and whether he,
and Grettir the Strong, and Illugi his brother, are
likely to be won thence against their wills."

"Now," cried Ondott, "I thank thee for this news.
And one in that land-side, Thorstein Angle, he is my
cousin; he will let me know if ever thy son comes
thence."

"If Thorstein Angle is thy cousin," said Asdis, "that
shows the saying true, that all rogues are akin. But if
thou hearest aught from that region, I pray thee let
me know if my son is well."

Now all the time Thurid sat there, and combed
no flax, nor said a word. "And yet," said Ondott, "I
hear that the woman works well at times."

"Speak not so loud in her presence," said Asdis,
"for methinks now she is tranced. Mayhap when she
comes to she will prophesy and tell me of my son."

"Nay," said Ondott, "the woman is clean daft, so
they say, ever since she left our house to wander in
the cold. Now who has split the wood that lieth
here, and piled it against the house? For thou hast
not done it."

"I will tell thee," said Asdis, and lowered her
voice. "On that night the frost got in her brain,
mayhap; for she was ever strange, but now she is
little short of marvellous. Sometimes she works
with a man's strength; and at such times she splits
wood, or carries water, or spades here in my little

field. I have done no heavy work since she came. But she is very silent, nor hath any save me and Frodi seen her face or heard her voice. Such is her mood."

"Now let us ride hence," said Ondott to Grani. "Asdis, I wish thee joy of thy mad-woman."

"Better live with her than alone," quoth Asdis.

So those men rode away, and they spread abroad the news that Rolf was gone from Broadfirth dales, for he was in Drangey with Grettir the Strong, and none could draw them from that isle. Steep were its rocks and high, to be scaled only by ladders, and three might hold the place against three hundred.

Word was also spread about of Thurid the crone: how she had fits of man's strength, and did work for Asdis. Men saw her going with great strides, or working in the field; at a distance she seemed taller than before, and bigger across the shoulders; but when one came near she shrank within herself. Moreover no one heard her voice now, save when she mumbled hoarsely.

Now on another day Grani rode to the settlement at Hvammferry, and on his way homeward came by the smithy of Frodi. Ondott was in his company, with Hallvard and Hallmund; they proposed that they should have sport with the smith, and take from him his bill.

"Sport mayest thou try," said Grani, "but beware lest it turn out against thee."

"He is soft as custard," quoth Ondott.

"Otherwise was he in the Orkneys," replied Grani. But for all that Ondott rode to the smithy-door, and called Frodi to come out. He came, and leaned on the handle of his hammer, which was so big that no man had wielded it since he went away. He asked what they would of him.

Said Ondott: "Here is Grani Earl's Fosterling to require something of thee."

Frodi said to him: "Was then Grani fostered by the Earl?" And he fixed Grani with his eye; but that one blushed and said naught. For he knew that his father had boasted of his fostering with the Earl, and never had Grani said nay thereto.

Asked Ondott, "Was he not?"

Frodi said, "He came last from the Earl's court." So Frodi, who might have spoken honor away from Grani, made him feel more shame than if the truth had been said.

"Now," said Ondott, "bring forth the bill which is Einar's, and deliver it to us."

"Asks Grani that?" Frodi replied.

Grani said, "I ask nothing." And he spurred his horse a few rods away.

Frodi went within the smithy and brought out the bill, but set also a helm on his head. Said he: "Here is the bill for whomsoever wishes it."

But Grani said over his shoulder, "Leave the bill with him. No use is it to us, for we have none that can wield it."

Then Ondott was wroth that Grani did not

support him in that claim, and he said: "Now, Frodi, I call to mind that ere thou wentest away, thou didst assault me here in this smithy. Outlaw will I make thee therefor."

Frodi made a sudden step, and behold! there he was within reach of Ondott, holding the bill in such wise that he might have thrust Ondott through, albeit Frodi neither raised the weapon aloft nor brandished it. He said:

"Now for the love which has always been between us, be so kind as to speak me free of guilt in that matter, when I drew weapon on thee."

In a fright Ondott stretched forth his hand and spoke Frodi free of that guilt. So Frodi suddenly shifted the bill in his hand, and the point touched the ground; none who had not looked close would have supposed any threat had been made. Said Frodi: "See how kind Ondott is to me, in asking no atonement, being in no danger from me. Witness ye all that I am clear in that matter."

Grani smiled and rode away, and the men next; Ondott followed, mightily vexed that that simple one had so bested him.

Now the time came for men to ride to the Althing, and with all state Einar rode thither with his son. Then for the first time Grani saw the power of that land which he had despised, for chiefs met there who were greater in riches than Orkney thanes, having great followings, all richly dressed. But all were obedient to the law; and a wonderful thing that was, to see men of such power yielding in lawsuits to lesser men, and bringing no cases to weapons. And Grani learned that his father was of no consequence at all in that place, for men passed him by and gave him no honor. Yet for all that Grani's pride grew, and he said that men should some day recognize him there. And he rode home moodily behind his company.

Now as men rode again toward the west, Grani saw one man whom he had oft remarked at the Thing: Kolbein the son of Burning-Flosi, destined to be a leader among men. Grani wished friendship with him greatly. And Kolbein rode to Grani and said: "Keeps thy father his harvest feast this year as before, asking company thereto?"

"Yea," answered Grani. "Wilt thou come?"

"Gladly will I come," answered Kolbein, "and will bring friends with me, if so be we shall be welcome."

"Welcome will ye all be," said Grani, and rode home cheered.

Now when they were come to Cragness, Helga met them at the door and welcomed them in. They asked if aught had happened in their absence. Said she, "Nothing save that the carline Thurid was here yestreen, and I am the first that has heard her speak since she left here in the spring."

They asked what were her words.

"I was here alone in the hall," Helga said, "for all the women were making cheeses in the out-bower. And Thurid came in and shuffled about the place, looking at things. I bade her be seated for I would bring her milk and oat-cake; but when I brought them she had the great bow in her hands, and looked at it but would not eat. So I set the food away again; and when I returned she had the bow and the quiver, and was near the door as if to take them away. She said nothing when I asked what she did with those; so I stood in her way, thinking I was stronger than she. With one hand she set me aside, and I might resist her no more than if she were a man. So she bore the bow and arrows from the house, and I thought they were gone; but on a sudden she was back again, and laid them on the bench. And she said in a deep voice not like her own:

" 'Not with women do I strive.'

"Then with great steps she went out of the hall, and came not again."

Those three, Einar and Ondott and Grani, looked at each other with alarm. For if that bow, left in the ward of women, had thus been taken, men could know neither the day nor the hour when Rolf might come, and make the shot at the oak-tree before witnesses, when all would be over with the house of Einar. And ere aught was said Einar took the bow and bestowed it under a settle, where it was well hid. Then they praised their fortune that they had it still.

So all sat down to meat, and ate gladly, for they had journeyed days long from the Thing-field. Then night fell, and they spoke of many things; at last Einar asked his son: "What said to thee Kolbein son of Flosi, there ere our roads parted?"

"He asked me," answered Grani, "whether we hold the harvest feast as last year, and if he and his company would be welcome."

Says Einar, rubbing his hands: "Now the great folk come to alliance with us; and when a few chiefs have visited here, then thou mayest count thyself their equal in all things, even as thou art in wealth. Of course thou badst him come?"

"That I did," says Grani.

So Ondott praised him. "Men have marked thee, there at the Thing, and seek to ally themselves with thee."

But Helga, who had listened, burst into tears.

"What is it," asks Grani, "that makes thee weep?"

Helga dashed the tears from her eyes, and stood before those two, her father and her brother. "Much had I hoped," says she, "that wicked doings would cease in this house—for to mock the dead and the unfortunate is wicked. And if ye hold the feast as last year, and shoot at the boundary as then, laughing at Hiarandi's fortune, then ye tempt your own fate, for such deeds go not unpunished long."

"Now," asked Grani of his father, "hast thou so mocked that luckless man's fate?" Einar said he had, and it was seen that Grani thought that act far too strong.

"Yet see," said Ondott, "what friends that brings you now, for from the house of Flosi comes this offer of friendship."

Now as they spoke someone knocked at the door, and there was a housecarle of Snorri the Priest.

"My master," said he, "passes on his way home from the Althing, and sends me to ask: hold ye your harvest feast as last year, and will he and his company be welcome?"

"Oh, hold it not!" cried Helga.

Then Einar turned to Grani. "The mightiest man in Broadfirth dales offers now his friendship, and thy future is sure. Shall we not hold the feast?"

Grani turns to the housecarle of Snorri, and says: "Beg thy master to come!"

XXVII

Odd Doings at Cragness

NOW TIME WEARS toward harvest, and in the dales all is quiet and busy, so that men when they meet have little gossip, save only of the doings of Thurid the crone. For she travelled far and wide in the night, and men saw her so distant from home that it was said she rode the wind; she was seen near the farm of Burning-Flosi, far to the east, and near the hall of Snorri the Priest, to the west. Ever when seen in the dark she strode furiously; by day she was always bent and slow. Old men spoke of her youth, when she was brisk and handy; it seemed as if her youth came again in these fits, foretelling her death.

Moreover by Asdis's work nothing now lagged, and the field was plowed, sowed, and harrowed, so that never had such a crop stood on those poor acres, and that by the work of two women. Some questioned whether indeed Rolf were not about; but there was no place in the hut for hiding a man, howbeit busybodies pried about there much. Now all that they found was what looked to be a grave,

not far from the home-mead. So then the tale ran
that Rolf was dead, and there buried; but when
questioned Asdis would only laugh and say:

"Whether it is a grave, or the place where stood
a little tree that I uprooted for fuel, that ye may
guess."

But she was always so blithe that it was sure her
son still lived.

Now on a day word came to Ondott from Thorstein Angle his cousin, that three men for sure
dwelt on the island of Drangey; they were Grettir
the Strong and Illugi his brother and some man
unknown; but whether more men dwelt there no
one could say, for so high were the cliffs that nothing could be seen from the mainland, and another
three might for a twelvemonth lie there hidden.
Many believed that others were there. So Ondott
was satisfied that Rolf lay in hiding there afar off,
and would not trouble the Cragness-dwellers for a
long time to come.

Now came harvest rich and full, a bountiful year;
men worked hard in the fields, the women too, and
at night sleep was sound. There came a morning
when it was found that Cragness had been entered
at night and the whole hall ransacked, its passages,
lofts, and store-rooms. Goods were taken from their
places and laid aside; chests had been moved, opened,
and emptied; and there was scarce a corner of the
place but had been searched. Yet gold and silver,
whether in money, rings, or vessels, were left behind,

nor were they even gathered together for booty. So it was seen that no common thief had been there, and men wondered wherefore that had been done.

But Grani sent all his men to work in the field, and the women to righting the house; then he took the bow from under the settle where it was hid with its arrows, and he thrust it within the dais whereon were the seats of honor.

Now a night passed again, and no one heard the dogs bark; but in the morning it was seen that the thief had come again, and all the settles were out of their places, as if one had searched beneath them. No other places were searched, and nothing had been taken; all thought it strange that the dogs had not barked. Then another day passed, and men came home to sleep as tired as before; so then Grani took the bow and hid it up under the thatch, when all had gone to their beds.

In the morning nothing had happened save that the seats on the dais had all been moved, and the dais was found set up against the wall. Now the dais was heavy, and that work had been done with much strength. While men were marvelling the neatherd came in, and said he had been awake early in the byre, with a sick calf. Before sunrise he looked out of the window; the light was not strong, but he could see a little way. There he saw the crone Thurid standing, near the house; but when he ran out to speak with her, she had moved toward the cliffs. Whether she saw or heard him he could not say, but suddenly she began to go with long strides. A little mist hung above the crags; into that mist she went, seeming to walk upon the air; and while he stood astonished the mist wreathed around her, and she was lost from sight. He said to himself that was the end of the old woman; but in an hour, looking toward the upland, he saw her walking to the hut of Asdis, and that matter he could not explain.

Grani sent all men about their work again; he took the bow from the hall, with its quiver, and carried them to the great store-house, and hid them beneath sacks of grain. Then a night passed, and nothing happened; but on the second night noises were heard; men took lights and searched in the hall, finding nothing. Yet in the morning it was seen that someone had been at work under the thatch of the hall, by every rafter; and it was a bold deed to do that ransacking in the dark, for a fall might mean death. No one had seen Thurid nor any living soul; yet a tatter of cloth was found, like as it had been torn from the old woman's gray cloak.

Now Grani takes the bow from the store-house, and thinks much by himself, and at last hides it in a haystack, an old one; and there the bow lies deep within. That night he sets men to watch in the store-house, and fetches dogs from a tenant's farm, and hopes now to catch the thief.

But one comes by night, and enters the store-house by the thatch, and takes the watchmen asleep, binding them with their heads in the bags that lay there. And all the store-house was searched and everything moved, and the thief away before day, but nothing taken. Those dogs which had been brought and tied by the door had had their leashes cut, and were off to their master; but the dogs of the place had given no sign. Those were the best watch-dogs in the dales, and had belonged to Hiarandi. No footprints were found about the place, and the watchmen said but one person had been there, marvellous silent and strong.

Grani took much thought where now to hide the bow, and bespoke the matter with Einar and Ondott; but they found no better place than where it lay, so there they let it bide. And Ondott went with men to the hut of Asdis, and called for the woman Thurid. Asdis said she slept within, and would not come out. So Ondott spoke to her from the doorway, as the crone lay within by the hearth; a bundle of rags she was.

"Is it thou that comest to our house," asked Ondott, "making this mischief there?"

"She speaks to no one save me," said Asdis, "and never when questioned."

"Tell her," said Ondott, "that if more searchings go on at Cragness, we will hale the old woman before the bishop and exorcise her for sorcery, since there must be witchcraft in these doings. So take heed to her, goodwife, and thyself as well."

"Thou art brave," said Asdis, "to threaten two women."

So Ondott rides away again, and that was the end of those happenings at Cragness. Some said the thief could not find what he sought; but some that Thurid was the thief, and Ondott had frighted her.

Time now fell for the harvest feast, and all preparations were made for receiving guests; great store of good things was made ready, and food and fodder for man and beast.

Comes at last Helga to Grani, and begs him not to hold the feast at all, for her mind misgives her because of it. He says that the guests must be on the way, and bids her work at the cooking, and forget those thoughts. She goes away sorrowful, and says no more of this to anyone.

Then on the morrow the guests are seen riding, both Snorri the Priest, that old man, and Kolbein, Flosi's son, each with a large company.

XXVIII

Of that Harvest Feast

NOW EINAR'S shepherd came in haste, and said the folk of the country-side were coming from all directions, and a great number would be at the feast. "Yet many," said he, "bear weapons, and I know not what that may mean."

So men looked, and it was seen that the farmers and bonders were coming over the hills, in small companies or large. Those of keen eyes said that most carried short-swords. Then Ondott looked at those two large parties that came riding, one from the east and one from the north, and thought them very numerous.

"Meseems," said he, "that Snorri and Kolbein bring more men than they need."

"Fearest thou, Ondott?" asked Grani. "This only do I fear, that we have not enough food ready. Only on going to church do men lay aside weapons; not strange were it if Snorri and Kolbein, coming from so far, bade their men bring longswords, spears, and shields. Yet they wear no mail, and bear only the one weapon—clear token of peace. Come, bid the women prepare more food; and do thou, father, let bring out more casks of ale, to welcome so many guests!"

Thus he shamed the household, and all went quickly to make ready more food and drink. Then the neighbors began to arrive, some on horses and some on foot, all in holiday guise save that each man bore a single weapon. Grani and Einar welcomed each as he came; and then the companies of those chiefs rode in, and there was great bustle to receive them. The horses were taken to the stalls, and the men led within the hall.

Gracious to Einar was Snorri the Priest, and he said fine words of Grani's growth and fair looks, and the goodly house. Kolbein was more silent, but looked about him much; and all those at Cragness were pleased with their great guests, save only Helga, who worked among her women and looked sad. When Grani saw that, he sought to cheer her, bidding her mark the pleasure of the visitors.

"Methinks," said Helga, "the old man smiles too much and the young man too little. Little good does my heart prophesy of this visit."

Grani was impatient with her and left her alone.

Now guests continued to come in, a great number, so many that they were not all able to come into the hall; those of lesser condition sat outside on the mead. And the time drew near noon before all were there. So at last Einar asked if more were to be seen coming, and his men looked abroad from the hilltop, and saw no one travelling. They saw only three living souls:

two were Asdis and Thurid where they worked in the garden by the little hut across the valley, and one was a great man who lolled on a nearer hillside and seemed to look out upon Broadfirth. Something glittered in the grass by his side, but no one knew who or what it might be. So Einar let call all forth from the house, and he stood on a stool, and spake to them.

First he bade them welcome, and then he spoke of that custom which the last year had seen begun: shooting at the boundary in memory of his owner-ship of those lands and that hall. Some, he knew, had been displeased thereat, yet he trusted that now they saw his reasons for it. "For in the sight of all," quoth Einar, "I will have it known that my title is just, and will prove that all which made me master here was done within the law."

Very reasonable was that speech; Snorri smiled and nodded graciously, and Einar's folk applauded, but the others not so much.

"Now," Einar said, "men claim that Grettir the Strong can make this shot and put me from my lands, but since the law allows no outlaw to meddle in suits, he may not make the trial. Yet I invite all other men hither to prove me guiltless; therefore come yet with me to the brook-side, and let all try who will. Few do I think will assay, but all are free to it. In token of peace leave your arms here, and let us go down to the boundary."

When they heard that, Einar's men laid aside what weapons they had; but those strangers made as

if they heard not, yet all together began walking to
the meadow by the brook. And Einar, when he saw
they took no heed to his request, was of two minds:
whether to say no more, or to ask again to lay aside
their swords. But that seemed a slight to his guests;
so he spoke not of it again, and all together they
went down the hillside, leaving at the hall only the
women, still cooking for so many people. Einar had
given orders that no ribald mocking should be made
in shooting, such as the baser of his men had done
before, for all should be decorous. So bows were
brought, the best there were; his bowmen made ready,
and one by one they shot before the guests. Snorri
sat on a dais which Einar had let make, and Kolbein
and Einar sat on either hand; but Grani stood. He
was very anxious to see how near the arrows would
fall to the oak; but the nearest fell roods away, and
he said to himself, "Now my father is completely
justified, for not even Grettir could shoot so much
farther than these men."

So he begged the visitors to shoot, and of Snorri's
men and Kolbein's some few made the trial, but shot
no better than those who assayed afore. Grani was
much pleased.

Then Einar stood up with smiles, and said he,
"Let us now go to the feast, for it is ready at the
hall."

"Here cometh one," said Snorri, "who may wish
to try; wait we here for yet a little while."

Men looked, and there was a great man coming

down the hill, and they knew him for the huge fellow who had been lolling across the valley. On his shoulder he bore a bill with a shaft big as a beam. Coming so, down the hillside above them, he looked so large that Einar was uneasy, wondering what champion he should be; the sun was behind him, and he seemed like one who might do all manner of feats of strength, even to making the long shot with the bow. Einar felt fear.

But when the large man reached the first of the people, and they could see his face, then laughter began among them, and one cried aloud, " 'Tis only Frodi the Smith!"

So Frodi came before them, and Einar was wroth because he had feared such an one, who was all softness. Said Einar: "What dost thou here with that great weapon at our feast, where no man comes in war? Seekest thou to take up the feud for this land?" And he gave sign that his men should be near, ready to seize Frodi if only cause were given.

But Frodi laid the bill at the feet of Einar, and said: "I bring thee the bill which is thine own, since it came ashore on thy beaches. As for that feud, it is not mine, but it belongs to the nearest of kin. Who knows where he is? Let me stay here a space, I beg, and watch the shooting."

"The shooting is past," said Einar, "but stay if it pleases thee. As for that bill, keep it for thine own, if it is at all dear to thee." Then he turned to Snorri, and said, "Shall we not go to the feast?"

"But tell us of this great bill," said Snorri. "And were there not perchance other heathen weapons which are thine, coming ashore in that great storm?"

So Grani told of the bill, how it had belonged to that dead viking; and he said there had been a bow with it, which was useless because no one could string it.

"Much would I like to see that bow," says Snorri.

Grani knows not what to answer and looks at Einar, and Einar looks back at Grani; but at last Einar says: "Old and useless is the bow, and it is in some out-of-the-way place. Come now to the feast, for it is all ready."

"It is not yet noon," answered Snorri, "and before noon I am never ready to feast. But here comes another one down the hill, who may give us sport until we sit down."

So men looked again up the hillside, and there was another figure coming, seen against the sun. (Now in Iceland, even in summer noon, the sun never stands overhead.) Fast the figure strode, all muffled in a cloak which flapped in the wind; and so wild and large did the newcomer seem that again Einar was afraid at the strange sight. But when it came near the figure dwindled, and the people laughed again, crying to make way for Thurid. With slow and halting step the crone came through the lane of men to Einar.

"Wishes the strange woman anything here?" asked Snorri.

"Give her money," said Einar to Ondott, "and bid her begone."

But she turned her back on Ondott with his purse, and went nearer Einar; and then she saw the bill which Frodi had left lying at Einar's feet. A strong shudder seized her, and there she stood shuddering, gazing beneath her hood at that great weapon.

"What is wrong with the woman?" asked Snorri as if impatient. "Bid her to speak."

"She speaks never," answered Einar.

But it seemed as if she were talking to herself, for first she began to mumble hoarsely, and then a little louder, and then at last she began to drone a song, in a cracked voice which, to those who had known her, seemed not her own. She sang thus:

> "Here is come from foreign shore,
> A heathen weapon and one more.
> First the bill which can be swung
> By the peaceful smith alone;
> Next the bow which can be strung
> Nor by him nor anyone.
> Yet I say in one of those,
> Laid in spells by Christ his foes,
> Danger lies to Einar's house."

When she had sung thus, she drew her hood still closer over her head and crouched down there by the dais.

Mark now all that which next was said and done, as if those visitors knew the fearsome nature of Einar, and played with it.

First Kolbein drew his feet away from the blade of the bill which lay before them; and he looked uneasy, saying to Einar: "Of human force I have no fear, but evil and witchcraft like I not."

But Snorri leaned forward and looked in the face of Frodi. "Tell us," says Snorri the Priest, "for what reason thou hast brought the bill here."

Answered Frodi: "I live alone in my smithy, and the bill stands always in the corner. Now sometimes it gives out a strong humming, there as I work, or as I sit by myself of nights; and at such times I think evil thoughts of vengeance, longing to do violence with the bill, until sometimes I fear I will snatch the weapon and rush forth and slay. And methinks the thing must be like the terrible bill of Gunnar of Lithend, which before every one of his slayings gave forth a singing sound. Yet Gunnar got his bill by the mere death of a man; but I won this in fight with a ghost, and so I fear more dreadful things will happen from mine than ever came from his. Lest blood-guilt come on my soul I brought the bill hither, to restore it to its rightful owner."

"But he gave it thee again," says Snorri.

"So," answered Frodi, "I see no way at all to avoid that blood-guiltness."

"Thou canst cast the bill in the sea," says Snorri.

On a sudden Frodi started back from the bill, and clutched at the clothes on his breast, and cried: "Heard ye how it hummed even then?"

Said Grani, "I heard naught."

But Kolbein hitched his stool further away from the bill, saying: "I heard something."

Snorri looked upon Einar, who was pale with fear. "Now," said Snorri, "what of that bow which, if shooting here at this boundary may cost thee thy life, is mayhap the greater danger to thee of the two?"

Einar answered nothing.

"Come," says Snorri, "do this if thou wouldst avoid all evil: cast this bill and that bow into the sea."

Now the crone rose up again, and she sang this song:

"Bring ye here those weapons forth.
Lay them crossing, east and north,
Here upon the fateful ground
Where death Hiarandi found.
Over them make ye the sign
Of the church, with holy wine.
Build ye then a fire great;
Ere the flames to coals abate,
Cast those weapons in them here.
Power of spells will disappear;
No fate then need Einar fear!"

"Now," said Snorri, "this burning is the best counsel, for weapons cast in the sea would come again to shore."

Then Thurid covered her head again and crouched down as before. But Einar rose in a panic and bade Grani fetch the bow, the arrows, and some wine. Grani departed hastily, and ran to the hall, and called his sister, bidding her bring wine while he get the bow and arrows.

"Now," cried Helga, "wilt thou mock the death of Hiarandi, and jeer at Rolf, who saved thy life here on the rocks?"

"What sayest thou of saving my life?" asked Grani.

Helga told how Rolf and Frodi had borne him to shore.

"Be comforted," said Grani. "No man shoots with the great bow, for Rolf, who alone can string it, is away. But witchcraft lies in it, and it shall be burnt. And when this feast is ended I will send for Rolf, and offer him peace and friendship."

"No peace comes from Rolf," answers Helga, "while we own his lands, nor friendship while we sit in his hall. Violence meets violence, so says the good book." But she went and got the wine, and Grani seized the bow and its quiver from out the rick, and bore all to the brookside again. There the fire was already built.

Snorri received the bow in his hands, for neither Kolbein nor Einar would touch it. The priest of Snorri's household took the wine, to hallow it; and Snorri drew the bow from its case.

"Let all give back," said he. "Make space for the fire and the burning of the bow. Let the crone say when all is ready."

So all men gave space; and the homemen and the guests, mingled together, made a great circle round the spot where the bow should be burnt with the bill. At only one place the ring was broken: the shelving bank of the brook, where men might not stand. Then Thurid rose and began to circle the fire. Thrice around it she walked, and Snorri with the bow came down from the dais and stood near; but Kolbein went and stood by Grani, and Frodi kept his place at the feet of Einar. So when the cloaked woman had circled the fire three times, she stopped and said to Snorri, "Give me the bow."

Snorri gave it her.

All watched to see what she would do, whether mutter spells or breathe upon it. But she looked at it carefully from end to end, and overlooked the string, and after that she raised it and shook it aloft. Then first men saw any part of her, namely her arm, which was not withered, but firm and large, like a man's. When she spoke her voice was no longer cracked.

"Water hath not harmed thee, oh my bow! Thou art the same as when thou slewest the baresark. Now shalt thou do a greater deed!"

And in a moment she set the end of the bow to her foot, and bent the bow, and slipped the string along, and the bow was strung! There stood the homefolk gazing, but the crone cast off the cloak. No woman was she at all, but Rolf in his weapons!

Then Frodi laid his hand on Einar's knee, and said:

"Sit still!" Kolbein set a knife to Grani's throat, saying: "Thy life if thou stirrest." And Snorri cried on high: "Where are ye, men of Tongue and Swinefell?"

All those guests drew their short-swords; and it was seen that by every one of the homefolk was a man of Snorri's or Kolbein's, or haply two of them. They threatened death to all of Einar's folk.

Rolf looked around on his enemies, and there was not one that could either fight or flee. So he took the quiver from Snorri, and looked within it; he chose that arrow with the silver point, and snapped the silken thread that bound it, and drew the arrow forth. At no man he looked, but up to heaven. Then he set the arrow on the string; he drew the bow and sped the shaft. High it flew, and far—across the brook, across the mead. It passed through the upper branches of the little oak, and fell to the ground three roods beyond.

Then in the sight of all Rolf bowed his head, nor for a while could he speak at all.

But when at last he turned again toward that high seat where Einar sat, his eye fell first on Ondott who stood by. Said Rolf: "Bring me that fellow here!"

Yet when they would seize Ondott he slipped away, and fearing death ran shrieking up the hill with men in chase. Such was his speed that they caught him not, so great was his flight that he recked not where he was going. He ran to the cliffs, nor saw them; from their top he fell and died.

"So is the greater villain gone," said Rolf when all

saw Ondott fall, "but the less remains. Einar, Ondott
hath made his choice of death and life; what choice
makest thou? Wilt thou bring this to the courts,
where outlawry is sure; or wilt thou handsel the case
to me, to utter my own award for the death of my
father and the seizing of my land?"

Einar said quickly: "On thy mercy I rely, and I
handsel all to thee, for I am too old to fare abroad."
So he came down from the dais, and hastened to
Rolf, offering his hand and calling Snorri to witness
that handselling. There they struck hands before all
those witnesses.

Said Rolf: "Now I hold in my hands thy death or
thy life, even as once thou heldest my father at thy
mercy. No pity hadst thou then. Shall I spare thee
now?"

"It was all Ondott's doing," said Einar.

"Now," quoth Rolf, "this do I award, and thy for-
getting it will be thy death. Thou shalt go to the
little farm where my mother has lived, but now she
is on her way to Cragness. On those few acres thou
shalt abide, and stay within all space a bow-shot
from it. The one ewe which is there thou mayest
have; the store of meat which is in the loft is thine;
my mother's gray cloak hangs by the door: take it.
But thine own livelihood thou shalt earn from the
soil when these are spent; and when thou comest
from thy boundary farther than this bow can shoot,
thy life is forfeit to me."

Einar accepted that award.

Then Rolf turned to Grani, and said:

"Grani, it lies in thy power to change all this by uttering two words."

Grani said nothing.

"Only two words," said Rolf again.

But still Grani answered nothing, and Rolf turned from him sadly.

"Proud is the heart of youth," quoth Snorri. "Come, let us sheathe our weapons. The sun stands at noon; now shall we execute the act of distress which will make Rolf master of his own—yes, and of the half of Einar's wealth, for the rest goes to the men of the Quarter. Let us go to the hall."

So all men went to the hall; and there went not only those guests from afar, but also those from the dales. Aye, and the men of Einar left him, and went to the hall with the others. Only Grani stayed with his father, and Helga whom anxiety had driven from the hall.

"Let us go to our new home," said Einar.

So they went, and from the first hilltop they saw how the act of distress was beginning at the crags; but from the second hilltop they saw that the act was finished. And when they rested on the long climb to the hut, whence Asdis had gone to her own old home, they saw how outside the hall men were seated at the long tables, and the women passed the food and drink, and all was merry at Cragness.

XXIX

Of the Trial of Grani's Pride

GAY WAS THAT harvest feast, and all men learned how Thurid had died in the snow on the night of the wreck. In her cloak had Rolf lived, serving his mother, and he had travelled to Tongue and Swinefell in order to make the plan for gaining his own; but because Flosi could not come he had sent Kolbein his son. Rolf gave great thanks to Snorri and Kolbein, and gifts besides; with all good wishes they parted on the morrow. Then Asdis took over the care of the household of her son, and Frodi was bidden to live there with them. They began again the custom of Hiarandi, to light beacons against shipwreck.

So now Rolf dwells at Cragness in his honor, but at the hut on the upland those others live with little ease.

Rolf looks out sometimes at the little farm, and sees Grani and his father working in the field to get in the small harvest, hay for the ewe and grain for themselves. Now for Asdis alone that store had been enough, but for three the outlook was not so good.

Once Frodi saw Rolf as he watched them work-ing, and the smith said, "Thou takest pleasure in the sight?"

Rolf asked, "Rememberest thou what jewels Grani wore, or his father, or Helga, that time when they went away?"

"Grani and Einar," said Frodi, "had rings on their arms and brooches on their breasts, but Helga wore none at all."

"Silver pennies also they had in their purses," said Rolf.

"What is their wealth to thee?" asks Frodi.

"Much," answers Rolf.

Now the time draws toward winter. The tale tells next how Rolf kept many people by him in the hall, to do the field work and to tend the cattle and horses (but the sheep were in the fold, save twenty which had not come in). Now some of those folk of Einar still dwelt at Cragness, having deserted their master, and none at the hall bade them either go or stay. Yet both Asdis and Frodi showed them little favor, and one by one they slipped away to seek livings else-where, save only those two, Hallvard and Hallmund, men of loud talk, strong of growth but not given to work. Evenings in the hall they spoke much, and Frodi scowled thereat; but Rolf sat in his seat and seemed neither to see nor to hear them.

Frodi said to him one day: "This one thing I mislike in thee, that thou keepest here those two who deserted their master."

Rolf asked: "Was their master worth devotion?"

"Maybe not," says Frodi, "yet ingrates are they both."

"They are free," said Rolf, "either to stay or go."

Frodi grumbled to himself, but said no more to Rolf.

Now October comes in very cold, but no snow as yet; and all harvests are in. Grani had stacked his neatly in ricks against the weather, for there was no room in the hut. There was a pen outside for the ewe; she was a good beast and never wandered, coming home at night.

On a day Rolf called Hallvard and Hallmund to him, and said: "It were not strange if Grani's ewe were to break out of its pen and eat at my ricks, which stand not far away." And he looked hard at Hallvard, who was the slyer of those two.

Said Hallvard with a grin: "That is likely to happen."

Rolf gave them each a piece of money, and said: "Beware of that ewe."

On a morning not long after came those two, leading the ewe. "Master, here have we found this ewe eating at thy ricks, nor know we whose it may be."

Said Rolf: "The ewe is Einar's. Take it to him, and ask payment for the hay which has been eaten."

So they take the ewe to Einar, and bring back silver. "Keep that for yourselves," Rolf said, "but will the ewe stay now at home?"

"Her pen is not strong," Hallvard said.

So on the morrow those two came again, bringing the ewe a second time; Rolf sent them for money as before. This time they brought back a gold arm-ring; so Rolf knew that Einar and Grani had taken with them nigh empty purses, and he was glad. He took the ring, giving the men silver, and said to them as before: "Will the ewe stay now at home?"

Hallvard answered, "We left Grani strengthening the pen, but still it is not high."

And on the morrow they brought the ewe, saying, "See how fat she hath gorged herself, master."

Then said Rolf, "Go now and say to Einar: 'A third time hath thine ewe trespassed; now must thou pay not only damages, but the trespass fine, or else bring this to the courts.'"

They went and brought back jewels, one arm-ring and two brooches; and Hallvard said, "All that he had Einar gave, rather than trust himself to the law."

Rolf gave them money, saying: "If the ewe wanders a fourth time, she will become mine. Is her pen strong?"

"Grani has no more wood to make the pen higher," answered Hallvard, "but he was tying her with a rope."

"Belike the rope is not strong," said Rolf.

And that seemed true; for on the morrow those two brought the ewe for the fourth time; they said she had again been eating at Rolf's ricks.

"Go now," said Rolf. "Say to Einar: 'Pay me damages and another fine, or yield thine ewe.'"

They went and returned, and said to Rolf: "The ewe is thine."

Then Rolf gave them silver rings, and they were well content. But Frodi came to Rolf, and said: "What is this thou hast suffered those two to do to thy neighbor? Now Einar will have no milk for the winter."

Rolf answered shortly: "He can use the pen of the ewe for firewood, and sell the hay for money." And he would speak no more of that.

Now October passed, and November came, and still there was no snow; the land was colder for that. One day when Rolf stood and looked at the hut on the upland, Hallvard came to him and said, "Small cheer is there over yonder, master; yet I have heard that Grani has sold his hay, and it is soon to be fetched from his farm."

Rolf answered: "See now how all their ricks stand in a line, and the wind is in that line, so that a fire which took the weathermost rick would burn them all. It was careless of Grani to set them so."

"For fire might come by chance," said Hallvard, and he went and spoke with Hallmund.

Now that night people were stirring in the hall, for a servingman was sick there; and in the early morning one came knocking at the door of Rolf's locked bed, crying, "There is fire across the valley." So Rolf threw on a cloak and went out; there was a great fire at the little farm, where the ricks were burning. In their light Grani was seen, saving what he might; but Einar stood by wringing his hands, and Helga weeping. So while those of Cragness stood and watched, Hallvard and Hallmund came up the hill and joined them.

"Where have ye been?" asks Frodi.

They had no good answer to give.

When it was day Rolf sent to inquire of Einar if he had had great loss; Hallvard was sent. "And ask if they will have any help of me; and mark how much they have saved and where it is bestowed."

So Hallvard went and returned again, and said that Grani needed no help. "But," said he, "the old man would have taken help, yet the young man would not allow it. And they have saved no hay, and but little grain; it is there in the pen of the ewe."

"Now," Rolf said privately to Hallvard, "thou and Hallmund shall take my shepherd and go into the hills, a day's journey; he shall show thee where are folded those twenty of my sheep which came not with the others, and which men call lost. Send him then home before thee, and do ye twain drive the sheep.—And see to it," quoth Rolf, "that those sheep do no damage to the fodder which Grani saved."

So that day those two took their staves, and went with the shepherd to do as Rolf had bidden. On the second day the shepherd came again; but on the fourth came Hallvard and Hallmund, driving the sheep. Now one of them was all bloody.

"What hath happened to the ram?" asked Rolf.

"We came home," answered Hallvard, "over the fell which is above Einar's farm; we pastured the sheep as we came, yet there is now no good grazing, and the beasts were terribly thin. So when we came late at night near to Grani's stead, and could not make Cragness in the dark, we rested and let the sheep stray. In the morning, behold, the sheep had found the grain which Grani had saved from the fire, and were eating the last of it when he came out by the first light. He saw the sheep, and drove them thence with fury; but the ram was obstinate, and would not leave the food, so Grani wounded him. And he gave us hard words before we gathered the flock to come away."

"Take the sheep to the fold," said Rolf, and he gave each of the men a piece of money.

Then he went in and sat down to meat; but Frodi followed him and seemed much discontented. "What ails thee?" asked Rolf.

"This ails me," said Frodi, "that thou hast no mercy upon them whose lot is hard enough. I cannot bear that thou shouldst use those base men to do such work against Grani, whom once thou lovedst. For I perceive clearly that all this has been done with intention, both the trespassing of the ewe and the burning of the ricks; likewise this last happening is not by chance. What change is on thee, that thou doest so?"

Also Asdis came and said: "Thou art hard on

those unfortunate ones, my son. Leave this persecution and do what is worthy of thee."

But Rolf said to Frodi: "Hast thou forgotten that Grani made thee thrall?" And of Asdis he asked: "Who slew Hiarandi my father?" The law of vengeance came to their minds, and they were silent, yet not satisfied.

Then Hallvard and Hallmund came in and helped themselves to meat, and began talking loudly. Said Hallvard, "Thou art called now, master, to avenge thy honor. Einar spoke shame on thee while we were gathering the sheep to drive from his house, for he said thou hadst the hope to starve him and his children."

"A great slander is that," quoth Hallmund, wagging his head. "Many a man hath died for such; and at least a money-fine should Einar pay."

"Hold your tongues!" cried Frodi in anger.

But Rolf rebuked Frodi, and said to those twain: "I give thanks for your thought of mine honor. But I do not desire blood, only money-atonement for the slander. Einar hath no money; but Grani hath yet his sword, a fine weapon. Now you who have my honor in your care, go to-morrow to Grani. Tell him I demand atonement; but if he sends me his sword his father's slander will be forgotten."

Those two looked at each other in doubt, for that would be a hard thing, to get from Grani his sword.

But Frodi sprang from his seat, and cried: "What

dost thou now, to insult Grani so? Never will an Icelander yield his sword! Call now to mind when ye two were comrades, and slept together, and fought the Scots together, and crossed the Pentland Firth together in a little boat, and swam the last mile side by side. Put all this in thy mind, and unsay what thou hast said."

Rolf answered: "All this I remember, and that is why I send for Grani's sword."

"Then," Frodi cried, "I leave thy roof now, nor ever are we friends again!"

"Frodi," answered Rolf, "sleep one night more under my roof; then if thou are minded thou shalt leave me forever."

Then Frodi called to mind his great love for his cousin, and yielded, and sat down.

In the morning Hallmund and Hallvard sat late at meat. Rolf said to them: "Why linger ye here? Do as I bade!"

Then they took swords, axes, and shields, and went to the hut across the valley, but had no heart in their going. Now Rolf watched from the hillside, and he saw them go into the farmyard, very slowly; and he waited a while, and saw them come out, very slowly. And they came back to Cragness, and climbed the hill to him; and behold, they had not their arms any more, but were wounded, and complained as they came.

"Grani," said they, "has done this to us. Now, master, avenge us on him!"

"Now," said Rolf, "all is come about as I wished." And he bade bring his sword and his shield.

"Wilt thou then," asked Frodi, "take up the quarrel of these wretched carles?"

Rolf put on his sword and took his shield; he made no answer to Frodi, but he beckoned his housecarles and pointed to Hallvard and Hallmund.

"Whip me," said Rolf to his servants, "these wretches from this place; if they wait till my return they shall feel the weight of my hand. But as for all the rest of you, bide ye here till I come again."

Hallvard and Hallmund ran with all haste away along the cliffs, but Rolf set out across the valley to the little farm.

XXX

Of the Saying of those Two Words

NOW THE TALE turns to speak of Einar and his two children: how they went away from their home with but the clothes on their backs, and with purses nigh empty, and but little jewelry. They came to the hut, to make a home where there was no room for a fourth to sleep, and where there was but a rack of dried meat, and a gray cloak hanging by the door, and little else for comfort. Grani looks about the farm, and sees how it has a good spring, and a small garden well tended, and a pen for the ewe. Beyond the garden were the other crops; yet the hay had not been cut, nor the grain reaped, and there was nothing stored against the winter.

Said Grani: "Rolf awaited this turn of fortune, and why should he lay up food for us?"

Then he turned about, and looked off from the hillside. There he saw Cragness, and the folk feasting; and he saw Fellstead and many other farms. There lay Broadfirth, and the sea beyond; fishing vessels were thereon. And he saw the ferry to Hvamm, with all the four roads which led to it, where people travelled; but the little farm was far away from all these things. Now it was a bright warm day, and the ewe bleated in the pasture, and the birds called each other above his head.

Then Grani's heart fainted within him, and he cried to Einar: "Better hadst thou chosen exile for us all, rather than condemn us to die in this place!"

Einar sought to excuse himself to his son, but appeased him not. Then Helga said: "Is this all thou didst learn in the Orkneys, thus to meet the fate which thou hast brought upon thyself?"

Then Grani was quiet, and went and fetched water, and wood which was there for the cooking (but there was no great store). After a while he said to his sister, "No more will I complain, though worse things come upon us."

So in the following days he sets himself to work, and cuts the hay, and stacks it in ricks; and cuts and stacks the grain likewise, working hastily lest the snow should come. Einar was of no account in such work, for his body was not used to it; but he watches the ewe upon the mead, and fetches water; and Helga works at the house, and when the grain is reaped she begins to grind it in a handmill; a slow labor that was, to make flour each day for their bread. Now when Grani had finished harvesting he began to cut peat and stack it near the house. It was hard work, for the cold was severe and the ground freezing.

Einar began to complain as the cold came on; he was not warm enough under the gray cloak, but sat much of the day by the fire. He disliked his food and wanted better, although naught better was to be had. It was not easy to bear his complainings; but Helga was patient, and Grani sought to lighten her labors, doing woman's work. Yet he was troubled for the shame of his life, and slept badly, and lost flesh. Now hard frost and bitter winds came, but still no snow. Grani's clothes were thin, and he was not used to the rough life; his hands cracked with the cold, all his joints ached, his feet were sore from his thin shoes, and it seemed as if he would perish with the wind. Yet still he cut peat, hewing it from the frozen ground in a little boggy place; and he brought it home with fingers all bleeding. Then Helga bewailed the weather, how without snow the ground froze ever deeper; but though at first Grani was minded to complain with her, he bethought himself and spoke cheerily.

Helga asked: "Why dost thou conceal thy thoughts?"

"The worst of my thoughts," said Grani, "are so bad that I dare not dwell on them. But the better is that I must be manly; and I have a memory to help me."

"What is that memory?" asked Helga.

So Grani told of that time when he and his thralls were lost in the snow in Orkney, and those two Icelanders bore the cold, but he complained of it. "And they gave me the cloak and the warmth of their own bodies, yet I could not be brave. So now when I shiver in the cold I call to mind their hardiness, and strive to copy it."

"That is well said," quoth Helga, "and I will show courage, even as thou."

So those two fortified each other; but Einar's mind dwelt always on his misfortunes: the great state he had lost, and the trick that had betrayed him, and all those servants who had deserted him. "Years long," said Einar, "I fed many of those men, yet they all turned from me at the end. Not one had the gratitude to follow me hither."

"There is luck in that," answered Grani, "for how could we feed them?"

"Most I hate Hallvard and Hallmund," said Einar, "for I favored them in everything, but now they cling to Rolf."

"He will get small profit from them," says Helga.

Now at the farm they took much comfort in their ewe, which never wandered far, and came home at night, sleeping always in the pen. But one morning she was gone and the pen broken down, and no trace of her was to be seen. Then Einar lamented greatly, since her milk was needed; he declared that she was stolen. But in the forenoon came those two, Hallvard and Hallmund, leading the ewe.

"This beast," said Hallvard, "was found eating from our master's ricks."

"Wherefore," asked Grani, "ate she not from our ricks, which were nearer?"

"I know not," said Hallvard, "but she hath been at our ricks; and Rolf has said: Twenty in silver must you pay."

Grani took his purse; and though his father scolded he gave silver, all that he had, and Hallvard and Hallmund went away.

Now this happened again, and to redeem the ewe Grani gave a gold ring. Then he built up the pen again of double strength, so that a bullock could not have broken out; but on another morning the ewe was gone, and unless she were a goat she might not have jumped out. Einar was terribly enraged with an old man's anger, and swore those two ruffians had killed the ewe; yet after a while they were seen coming, leading the beast.

Einar said to Grani, "Take now thy sword and slay them when they come."

But Grani held his tongue and heard those two quietly when they claimed trespass money; he gave them all the jewels that he had, and the twain went away. Then Einar cried, "I have no son at all, but two daughters; and no one will defend me from this shameful persecution."

Grani grew red as blood; but he said naught in answer, and tied the ewe in the pen. When he was alone Helga came to him.

Asks she: "Thinkest thou that the ewe broke out those two times, and leaped out the third?"

He answers: "Those two stole her, yet I cannot prove it, for there is no snow to show their tracks."

"I blame not thy mildness at all," says Helga, "rather do I praise it. But why art thou so quiet under injustice?"

"I call to mind," says Grani, "that when I enthralled Rolf he never complained, but took what fortune brought him, seeing that he could not help himself. He bided his time and avenged his father; and I suffer in silence, to keep my father alive. That lesson which Rolf set me, now I follow; I cannot resist him, save to my death, and what then would become of my father and of thee?"

Now there came another night, and in the morning the ewe was gone; that day Grani yielded her to Rolf, as already told, while Einar upbraided him that he was so unmanly. And in the next days the old man was miserable, missing his milk, and not eating the broth Helga made, though the broth was very good. He made himself sick with his anger and his selfishness, and went to bed in the middle of the day, and scolded from where he lay. "Men tell," said he, "of Gisli the Outlaw, who entered his enemy's house and slew him for the slaying of his blood-brother. But nowadays no man will do such a deed —no, not to save his father."

Then Grani started from his place, and said: "Violence enough has been done in this feud, nor will I ever have hand in such." He went out of the house, and Helga after him.

She said to him: "Be comforted, my brother."

Grani answered: "It is true that I might take Rolf

unawares, and slay him. But I remember when he was my thrall in the Orkneys, going with me everywhere, and my life was daily in his hands. For when we were on the cliffs he might have cast me down, and no man would have known he did it. Or when we were fishing he might have drowned me, and have sailed away in the boat. But he never did evil for evil, and I remember it now."

Then Grani planned to sell his fodder, and the money would be welcome. But on another morning they woke in the hut with the crackle and glare of fire, and there were the ricks burning, all of them; Grani could save little from the flames. Now that was a great loss, and Einar bewailed it, saying that since the wheat was gone they would all three starve. Then by day they saw Hallvard coming.

"He comes to insult us," said Einar, and egged Grani on to meet him with his sword, and wound him for punishment. But Grani received Hallvard mildly, and said he had no need of help, and sent him away.

"Now," said Einar, "we might have had help of Rolf, and thou hast refused it."

Grani answered naught to his father, but afterward when Helga asked why he sent Hallvard away, Grani said, "What help gave we to Rolf when he was shipwrecked at our door? Thou savedst his life, else he had been slain in our hall. For very shame we can take no help of him."

Now some days passed, and Einar grumbled ceaselessly, so that life with him was well nigh unbearable; yet he was the cause of all their misfortune. In nothing that she did might Helga please him; and though Grani had grown thin with labor, his father did not spare the lash of his tongue. It was plain that they had not enough food to keep them through the winter, now that so much grain was gone, and their fate was much on Grani's mind; yet he was cheerful.

Helga came to him at last, and said, "Brother, give me of thy courage, for with my father's harshness and our hard work I feel my heart failing me. On what thought dost thou sustain thyself?"

"Dost thou remember," asked Grani, "that when we first came here I complained, and thou didst ask: Had I learned no more in the Orkneys than to bewail my fate?"

"Forgive me that saying," begged Helga.

"Why not forgive?" Grani said. "For I was reminded of a boast I made to Rolf there on the cliff by Hawksness, saying that I feared no misfortune. And he answered: Then I was fitted to be an Icelander. Then, though I had dwelt so long in the Orkneys, my heart warmed to my own land whose children love her so; and I resolved to show myself an Icelander, for the sake of winning Rolf's praise. Therefore I strive, my sister, to be a true son of this dear Iceland, and to bear my misfortunes even as Rolf sends them."

"Mayhap," says Helga, "Rolf remembers also that boast of thine."

"Aye," says Grani.

"And mayhap," Helga says, "he sends these trials only to test thee, for it is clear that they are of design."

"So I have thought," Grani answers. "Either it is that, or it is revenge; yet Rolf has no spite in him.

"Greatly dost thou praise him," Helga says.

"Not overmuch," quoth Grani. "And now I will say I repent my pride when I refused his friendship: first at Hawksness, when he had done me that slight hurt, and then on the ship. But I have most shame that I offered him no atonement when I was prosperous here in Iceland, and he was in hiding."

"Go to him now," cries Helga. "Ask forgiveness!"

Grani answers: "I asked it not when I might with honor; it were cowardice to do so when I am under his feet."

Now Helga wished to argue against that; but their father called them, complaining, and there was no more of their talk. But Grani, while Helga tended on Einar, ground corn in the handmill (but there was little of the grain left) and sang this song:

> "Once I, most fortunate,
> Met swords in fight.
> Now, sin to expiate,
> I show this plight:
> Grind corn to make my bread.—
> Evil pursues my head."

And it seemed to him that scarce ever had a warrior, not in thraldom, come to such fortune. Then when he had ground enough meal for another day he stacked the grain carefully against the weather, and went about other tasks, and that night slept soundly.

But in the morning, waking with the first light, he heard as it were a scuffling of feet close outside the door; when he opened he saw sheep there, a small flock, eating eagerly at the grain, which was almost all gone. In despair he rushed out upon them, and drove them away; they all fled before him but one lean old ram, who stood his ground and still would eat. Then Grani took a club and smote the ram, and wounded it, so that it ran away. Next he saw how at a little distance were Hallvard and Hallmund, who came and excused them of the doings of the sheep, which had strayed while the men slept. Grani answered nothing, though his sister wept; but Einar was nigh out of his mind for anger and despair, and cursed those twain, and Rolf their master, until Grani took him and led him into the house, when those two drove the sheep away. Einar was so spent with rage that he fell at last in a stupor; and Grani went and gathered all that remained of the grain. There were but two measures of it left.

Then as he gleaned those few stalks from the ground, where the sheep had trodden them, and as he cleansed them of dust and saved every small particle: bitterness grew in him, and then wrath, and he nursed his wrath all that day. Now Helga was busy with her father, and saw not how Grani brooded; there was not much food for him, but he fed on his despair. And he slept ill that night, and rose early, and went without food to dig in the garden for roots. There those twain found him, Hallvard and Hallmund, when they came into the yard that day for his sword.

Now his back was toward them, and they asked each other: "Shall we rush on him and wound him, or slay him, and so search the place at our will for his sword?" That seemed to them the best counsel and they stole upon him. He was so busy that he heard them not; and but for Helga he had been slain. But she saw the men, and cried "Beware!" So Grani turned with his spade uplifted, and they rushed at him. Then he dashed the sword from the hand of Hallmund, and struck fiercely at Hallvard. Hallvard he wounded with the spade, but Hallmund with his own weapon, and with their wounds they limped away.

Then all of Grani's anger left him, and he sat in the house by the hearth, and his father waked and looked at him. Said Grani, "Much didst thou do to Hiarandi for my sake, and harshly has Hiarandi's son repaid me for thy sake. But let us forgive each other, father, before the end of life comes to us."

Asked Einar: "How comes the end of life now?"

Helga says from the doorway: "I see Rolf coming across the valley, and he is armed."

"Thus comes the end," says Grani, and they embraced and kissed each other all three, and Grani made ready for death, and he went out to meet Rolf. Rolf came into the yard, and he had his sword and shield.

Says Rolf: "What hast thou to say to me for the wounding of my housecarles?"

Grani looked on Rolf, and remembered how he had loved him once, and loved him still, yet never might they be friends. "This offer will I make," said Grani. "I will fare abroad, and never come back to trouble thee, if so be thou wilt give my father, while he lives, his winter's food."

"Hast thou nothing better to say?" asked Rolf.

"I will make this offer," said Grani. "I will be thy thrall, and labor for thee, if only thou wilt maintain my father out of thine abundance."

"Canst thou say no better?" asked Rolf.

Grani remembered how he might have been friends with Rolf, and would not; and how he should have asked forgiveness, and could not. "Nothing better to offer have I," said he. "Nothing worth offering." For he despised himself, and thought his life ended.

"Take then thy weapons," said Rolf, "and fight me here on the level space by the spring."

So Grani took his sword and his shield, and they stood up to fight by the spring, and those in the hut heard the clash of steel. The two looked strangely fighting, Grani gaunt and ragged, and Rolf well fed and in holiday clothes. Now Grani thought to be slain quickly; but Rolf seemed to have no power at first; yet he warmed to the strife, and began to strike manfully, and at last he smote away a part of Grani's shield. Then Grani by a great stroke shore away the half of Rolf's shield.

"Well smitten!" cried Rolf, and they fought on; but Grani found himself growing weak, and marvelled much that Rolf smote no faster. "But if he means to tire me out," thought Grani, "he can win me easily."

Then Rolf drew away, and said: "My shoestrings are loose, I will tie them." So he laid aside his shield and sword, and knelt before Grani to tie his shoes; Grani might have slain him there, but he waited. And not to be tempted to that treachery, Grani looked about; he saw the hut where were his father and sister, and looked off on the firth and the wide land, and waited for Rolf to rise. Then they fought again.

But Grani grew weary and desperate, and his thoughts grew hard. For there were his sister and father close at hand, and the world was beautiful. And while they fought slowly he thought that cruel, so to prolong death, since for Rolf he was no match at all. He wished for death, and exposed his breast to Rolf's strokes, and cared not what happened.

But Rolf drew away again, and said, "I am thirsty," and knelt down by the spring to drink. Then in his great weariness Grani gave way to an evil thought, and cried, "I will free my father, even if the deed be foul." And he heaved up his sword to slay Rolf.

But Rolf rose upon his knees, looking fair in Grani's face; and though Rolf made no defence,

Grani stayed the sword in midair, and cast it far away. Then he sat down on a stone and covered his face with his hands.

Rolf rose, and came to him, and said: "Wherefore didst thou not slay me?"

Grani answered: "Because once I loved thee."

"Grani, Grani," cried Rolf, "has thy pride at last come to its end? Now once more I ask: What hast thou to say to me?"

"For the wounding of thy henchmen, and for all I ever did to thee since first we met," said Grani, "only this I beg: Forgive me!"

"I forgive thee!" Rolf cried, and there they embraced and made peace.

This is the end of the tale, that Frodi slept yet other nights at Cragness than that one, and lived with Rolf his life long. But Grani took his father home to Fellstead, and dwelt there, he and Einar and Helga. Grani was ever the greatest friend of Rolf, but Einar never came into Rolf's sight so long as he lived; and that was not long, for the old man was broken with his shame. Then after that Rolf took to wife Helga the sister of Grani, and the curse of the Soursops never troubled their children. Between the households of Cragness and Fellstead was ever the closest bond, and famous men are come of both Rolf and Grani.

So here we end the Story of Rolf.

Glossary

Althing — the Icelanders' parliament or congress, where men gathered to make laws

Baresark — a frenzied fighter of a traditional type among the Norse (forerunner of "berserker," one who goes berserk)

Byre — cow barn

Carline — an old woman; a hag, a witch

Chapman — a trader

Churl — peasant

Dight — to equip

Dolt — a slow, dull-witted person

Firth — a narrow inlet of the sea

Fostering — bringing up of a youth in a family other than his own

Hag — an ugly, vicious old woman; a witch

To handsel — to give into the hands of another; as a noun, a gift

Hest — bidding, behest, order

Hight — to be called, named

Holm, holmgangs — a holm is an islet; a holmgang is a duel to the death; going, or challenging, to the holm means going to the place (the islet) where the duel would be fought

Mere — lake; arm of the sea

To put out at call — to invest

To reck — to be concerned

Rede — advice; interpretation

Rood — a linear measure of around six to eight yards

Skald — Scandinavian poet of the Viking period

Thane — a person of rank

Thole-pins — pins set vertically in the gunwale of a boat, serving as the fulcrum for the oars

Thrall — a slave

Wether — a castrated male sheep

Wore — from "to wear," to veer, or turn a ship about by swinging its bow away from the wind

About the Author

ALLEN FRENCH (1870–1946)

Allen French was a careful, scholarly writer of history. Several of his historical works on the Early American period are still in print today. More than once he traced undiscovered primary sources which shed new light on the happenings of the American Revolution. Yet, meticulous as he was, history was always to him more than dry facts. Whether Allen French was writing scholarly works or exciting tales for boys, his endless fascination with the past allowed history to come alive. His wife, Aletta, once wrote that while deeply immersed in what was to be his final major historical work, *The First Year of the American Revolution,* her husband also wrote a children's book on the Romans in Britain and a novel about the Puritan Migration to America. She says, "His imagination fired his mind to the point where it blazed and he would take to fiction to let off the heat!"

She further writes, "I think there were two elements in his devotion to history. One, a deep desire to proclaim the truth, avoiding no damaging details and letting the honors fall where they might. The other an enthusiasm for the drama of history which required heroes and villains and all the 'props,' and which logically led to stories of knighthood and chivalry such as *The Colonials, Sir Marrok, Grettir the Strong, The Story of Rolf and the Viking's Bow, The Red Keep* and *The Lost Baron.*"

Long-time family friend and author, T. Morris Longstreth, writes of Allen French, "It was hard for him to sit through a meal without our talk driving him to the encyclopedia. Yet there was no pedantry in all this, but rather a sense of adventure, the same romantic sense that led him to write his boys' books. History was for him a living glory."

Once he and his wife spent six weeks near Vézelay to gather "color" for *The Red Keep*, set in Burgundy in the twelfth century. He wrote: "Of the writing of history I have only this to say: that as my fiction was constructed out of imagination guided by common-sense, my history is common-sense illuminated by imagination. Common-sense: one should always be controlled by the facts of the case, ascertained by the most careful study, and set forth fairly to both sides. And imagination should try to make the facts living and interesting — not romantic nor sensational, but human." He finishes by saying, "If a man takes his work seriously, and himself not too seriously, he has a good chance of doing something worth while."